PRAISE FOR JULIE SMITH AND HER REBECCA SCHWARTZ MYSTERIES

"An interesting new detective personality . . . Smith shows an Agatha Christie-like capacity for making much ado about clues, concocting straw hypotheses, and surprising us, in the end. . . . Smith's crisp storytelling, her easy knowledge of local practices, and her likable, unpredictable heroine will make readers look forward to more of sleuth Schwartz's adventures."
San Francisco Chronicle

"A delightfully modern sleuth."
Minneapolis Tribune

"Rebecca's lively first-person narration brands her a new detective to watch."
Wilson Library Bulletin

"An attractive and amusing heroine."
The San Diego Union

THE SOURDOUGH WARS

Julie Smith

IVY BOOKS • NEW YORK

Ivy Books
Published by Ballantine Books
Copyright © 1984 by Julie Smith

All rights reserved under International and Pan-American Copyright Conventions. Published in the United States by Ballantine Books, a division of Random House, Inc., New York, and simultaneously in Canada by Random House of Canada Limited, Toronto. Originally published by the Walker Publishing Company, Inc. in 1984.

Library of Congress Catalog Card Number: 83-40424

ISBN 0-8041-0929-X

Printed in Canada

First Ballantine Books Edition: December 1992

For Betsy Petersen, without whom none of this would ever have happened.

The author wishes to thank several people whose advice was invaluable in writing this book: Megan Annand on law; Leo Kline on sourdough theory; Ralph Salaices on sourdough practice; Jon Carroll and Felicity O'Meara on geography. If any tiny liberties have been taken with facts, it is absolutely not the fault of these good people. Nor are any of the characters in this book meant to resemble them or anyone else. The same goes for bakeries and baking families: All depicted herein are wholly fictitious.

CHAPTER 1

Chris Nicholson, my law partner, had a nine o'clock court date on Monday. When she straggled in around eleven, our secretary greeted her with his accustomed politeness: "Been gettin' any lately?"

Male secretaries are quite the thing nowadays. Lots of lady professionals revel in them. They wear fashionable narrow ties and button-down shirts. They type a zillion words a minute, they take shorthand, they dust, make great coffee, and run beautifully oiled offices. That was the story I was hearing from some of my friends, anyway.

Ours dressed sloppily, made lousy coffee, couldn't take shorthand, typed about forty words a minute, and never remembered to give us our messages. His name was Alan Kruzick, and he was my sister Mickey's boyfriend. Also a starving actor.

Mom had talked us into hiring him after Mickey finished her master's and got a job at Planned Parenthood in San Francisco. Mickey and Kruzick had moved from Berkeley to the city so she wouldn't have to commute, and their rent doubled. None of us Schwartzes liked the idea of Mickey's supporting Alan—and Mom thought her little idea was the perfect solution.

So far as I was concerned, he wasn't working out, but Chris was a sucker for his smart-aleck style. Also, she was in a very good mood that Monday morning, so when he asked if she'd been gettin' any, she said, "Bet your booties, baby.'' Then she whipped into my office and sat down.

"Very businesslike," I said.

"Oh, who cares. No one's here."

"How was your weekend?"

"I spent it with Peter Martinelli. I think I'm in love."

"Oh, Lord. How many times did you have to sit through *Sleuth*?"

"I washed my hair during performances."

"Very convenient. When's the wedding?"

"First we have the auction. Then we worry about the wedding."

"What auction?"

"We're going to auction off the sourdough starter—like Alan suggested."

The previous Friday night, Chris and I had gone to the Town Theater with Mickey and my friend Rob Burns, to see Alan play Milo Tindle in *Sleuth*. Andrew Wyke, the wronged husband bent on revenge, was played by the elegant Peter Martinelli, scion of a once-great sourdough dynasty. Afterward, Alan and Peter joined us for drinks.

The play put us in the mood for S. Holmes, Esq. (or "the Sherlock Holmes pub," as it's usually known). This is an odd watering hole at the top of the Holiday Inn at Sutter and Stockton, but it's not nearly so odd as the hotel's doorman. Or, rather, as his appearance. He's a heavyset, elderly black man wearing an Inverness cape and deerstalker cap.

The pub itself features deep plush chairs and sofas, dozens of large-bowled meerschaum pipes in display cases, and a very good replica of the great sleuth's Baker Street digs. Despite its delightful appointments, it's hardly ever crowded, though it isn't *that* hard to figure out why: S. Holmes, Esq., is insanely expensive. Of course Kruzick suggested it, and of course he knew we'd have to treat him to celebrate his triumph on the boards. That's Kruzick for you.

Chris and Peter Martinelli ended up sitting next to each

other, and both of them seemed pretty happy about it. Each was tall, each was slender; she was light, he was dark. I didn't know a thing about him, but she was on the rebound from a long-term romance.

Chris and I used to call her former lover "the perfect man." Larry was sweet, gentle, a good cook, a successful architect, a looker—what more could you ask? "A little backbone," Chris said after the breakup. "He was a no-growth stock."

Larry was a little older than we were, and he wanted to get married. Chris didn't; and she reasoned that if he'd really been perfect, she would have wanted marriage. So she dumped him and started looking around for someone perfect. At the moment, she had her blue eyes firmly fixed on Peter Martinelli. I decided to help her out.

I fixed my own eyes on him. "Hey, handsome," I said, "are you married?"

He shook his head. "Never have been." He looked at Chris: "And I'm a great catch, too."

"Do tell."

He laughed. "I'm kidding. What you see is what you get. I haven't got a penny."

"You can't kid me," said Kruzick. "You've gotta have bread bucks."

"Being a Martinelli," said Peter, "doesn't even get you a good table at a restaurant anymore."

The famous Martinelli Bakery, the oldest and by far the best of the old-time sourdough producers, had had to close down a few years back. It was the old story—a small family business that expanded too fast, hit a recessionary period, and got in too deep. A few years after it went bust, the elder Martinellis—Peter's parents—were killed in a mudslide. Every San Franciscan knew the story.

"Oh, come on," said Kruzick. "There must have been a house or something. Stocks and bonds, maybe."

"No stocks, no bonds. My sister got the house."

"Didn't you get anything?" Kruzick can be unbelievably obnoxious, but somehow he gets away with it.

"Sure I did. I got the starter."

"Huh?"

"When my folks closed the bakery, they never gave up the idea that they'd be able to reopen it some day. So they had the starter frozen. You know what cryogenics is?"

"Sure," said Kruzick. "It's like in *Sleeper*, when Woody Allen dies and has himself frozen. Then he thaws out in the next century or something."

Peter shrugged. "That's what they did with the starter. Got a cryogenics firm to freeze it, just in case. At that time, there *were* some stocks and bonds. Dad thought he could sell them and borrow some money, maybe get some investors. . . ." He shrugged again. "But he never got it together."

"So you got the starter."

"Yes."

"Well, what's that?" Kruzick is from New York and harbors pockets of ignorance.

"It's what you need to make sourdough," said Rob. "San Francisco's unique sourdough French bread," he continued, "is the stuff of myth and legend. Yet the Martinelli loaf, with its familiar thick, dark crust and chewy, fragrant interior, was the acknowledged pride of San Francisco bakeries, a legend unto itself."

"Hey," said Peter, "I remember that. That's what the *Chronicle* said when the bakery closed."

"I know. I wrote the story."

"But what's the starter?" said Kruzick.

Rob went on quoting himself. "Sourdough first surfaced during the Gold Rush of eighteen-forty-nine. Perhaps the forty-niners brought it with them; maybe they developed it here. No one knows for sure. Some say the city's cottony fog gives the bread its sour taste; some say there's a certain yeast that grows only in San Francisco. But one thing is certain— you can't make it from scratch. You have to have sourdough to make sourdough."

"I think," said Kruzick, "I'm catching on."

Rob nodded. "A mixture of flour and water called the

mother sponge, or the mother sour, is the starter you need before you can bake your bread. Each bakery 'builds' its starter several times a day by adding more flour and more water to a portion of it, which must then rise and rise again. Each rising takes seven hours. And then the loaves are popped into the oven.''

"So what's so special about this dough sponge?"

"It's just one of those ineffable things," said Mickey. That was the way she usually handled Kruzick—by using words he couldn't understand.

"It is indeed," said Rob. "The bread's only as good as the mother sour.''

"So *is* there a special yeast?" said Mickey. "Or what?''

"It's said that the old-time bakers used to make the loaves by shaping the dough in their armpits," said Rob. "And that's what gave it its special flavor.''

"Oh, quit teasing us.''

"Well, there *is* a special yeast." He was talking like himself again. "It's called *Saccharomyces exiguus*, but you can find it lots of places. The Italians use it to make panettone, for instance. It's the reason the bread takes so long to rise— it's what scientists call a poor gasser.''

"But if they have it in Italy," asked Chris, "why can you only get sourdough in San Francisco?''

"Ah, because you also need a bacterium that really is found only around here. It's called *Lactobacillus sanfrancisco*. During the long rising, a sugar called maltose is formed. The bug works on the maltose to form two acids— seventy percent lactic and thirty percent acetic, which gives the bread its sour taste. Other bacteria won't produce that much acetic acid, and other yeasts won't tolerate that much. So you need both to make sourdough.''

"So, Peter," said Kruzick, "you gonna start a bakery?''

Peter shook his head. "I'm lousy at business. Listen, I'm a starving actor. I live on what I make from commercials.''

"How about if the theater paid you a salary?''

"Ever since the state funds got cut, the theater can't even pay for parking."

"But suppose someone established a foundation for the theater, and the foundation paid you a salary? I mean, someone who knew about the plight of the theater and wanted to save it—someone, say, who'd make a great artistic director. We're gonna need one when Anton leaves. You'd be great."

"I've applied for the job. The only thing is, there's probably not going to be a job. The theater's not going to last long and you might as well get used to it, Alan."

"So why don't you save it?"

"I don't have any money." Peter turned out his pockets. "What does it take to make you believe me?"

"What I mean is, why don't you auction off your starter?"

We were on our second drink by that time, and no one was thinking too fast. Everyone was silent for a moment.

Peter spoke, finally. "No one but my sister ever wanted to buy it, and I'd sell it to Russia first."

"No one knows how valuable it is, so we've gotta tell 'em. See, here's what we do. We make it a media event. We get Rob to write a story about you and how you're trying to save the theater. You announce publicly that you're going to auction off your starter, and Rob writes some purple stuff about how great the Martinelli bread was. And you invite people to bid."

We stared at him.

"They'll come running."

"I think it's a great idea," said Rob. "I love that old sourdough stuff. I could write about it day and night."

"Then when we get the money," said Kruzick, "we'll build this great new theater—and we'll have guest artists and everything, plus our own company, in original plays by local playwrights."

"You get to be the star of every play," said Mickey. "Because it was your idea."

Like I said, we were on our second drink. So it went on that way for a while. We had a high old time planning rosy futures for Alan and Peter, but no one took it seriously. Chris and Peter hardly listened. They just kept touching each other whenever they made conversational points. If you ask me, they had only one thing on their minds.

CHAPTER 2

"Chris, listen," I said. "Forget this auction idea. The moon was full last night. You're just feeling a little funny, that's all. It'll go away in a day or two."

"Think about it, Rebecca. What's wrong with it? Pick holes in it. Really try."

I thought about it. I really tried. And I couldn't come up with any objections. "I guess," I said, "the worst that could happen is it might not work. I mean, maybe no one will want to bid."

"Exactly! And what harm would that do? None. Listen, Peter wants us to set it up. He's our client."

"He doesn't need a law firm. He needs a business manager or a financial consultant. Something like that."

"He wants us."

"He wants you."

She patted her hair. "The things I do to get clients."

"Oh, stop. He's really serious about our setting it up?"

"Yes."

"Then I guess we'll have to consult a consultant." I picked up the phone and dialed a friend who was one and who owed me a favor. He told me exactly how to do it, and I told Chris. Then I called Rob to see if he still wanted to do the story. He said he'd get back to me, and he did, in five minutes.

"The city editor loves it," he said. "Thinks it's the greatest *Chronicle* yarn since sliced muffins."

"Don't you mean sliced bread?"

"Rebecca," he said, "your brain's going. Don't you remember the sliced-muffin story?"

"Can't say that I do."

"It was in 1967."

"I was too young at the time. Refresh my memory."

"There's nothing worse than a sliced English muffin, you know what I mean? You've got to tear them apart, so you get a nice uneven surface with big craters for butter to drip into."

"So?"

"So the local English-muffin makers started slicing the goods. We ran it on the front page for a week. In the end, they went back to the good old way. Hottest story since 'A Great City Forced to Drink Swill!' "

I did remember that one—or at least I remembered hearing about it. I was a tyke at the time. The *Chronicle* had exposed the fact that city restaurants were serving terrible coffee. That was it—the whole story. It was the greatest little circulation booster of the decade. That was the kind of city San Francisco was and the kind of morning paper it had. So of course the city editor went bonkers for sourdough.

The story ran the next day, in a wiggly-rule box above the fold on page one. The box also contained a mouthwatering three-column picture of a sourdough loaf broken open so you could see the famous dark crust contrasting with the tempting chewy interior. I bet everyone in the city had sourdough for lunch that day, and those who didn't had it for dinner. But then, that was about the way San Franciscans ate on an ordinary day. Sourdough with fresh salmon. Sourdough with cracked crab. Sourdough with shrimp Louie, chef's salad, pasta, petrale sole. Burgers on sourdough rolls. My mind was wandering, and I mentally congratulated Mr. City Editor. This was bigger than sliced muffins. It might be the biggest thing since the earthquake.

Rob's story made Peter sound very naive and charming. It outlined the history of the Martinelli Bakery, referred movingly to the tragic death of Mom and Dad Martinelli, and portrayed the youthful Peter as a sensitive child who never had any interest in business, much to the despair of his parents. He had been an artistic child from the first, and his teachers had recognized his talent, but the Martinellis had done their best to squash it and turn him into a baker. Peter had suffered enormous guilt when Mom and Dad died, but, as he put it, "that didn't make me any smarter in business." So he had pursued his acting career, and Rob mentioned three or four local triumphs and a couple of movies he'd been in. The story ended like so:

" 'I don't know if anybody'd really be interested in buying a frozen batch of dough,' said Martinelli. 'But I thought I'd give it a try. Unless some money comes in from somewhere, the Town Theater's going to have to fold, and I like to think it's been kind of a cultural enrichment to the city. So I just thought I'd try. If anybody wants to bid, they can contact my lawyer, Chris Nicholson. I don't guess they will, but just in case.' "

I didn't really approve. From what I'd seen of Peter Martinelli, he wasn't really an "aw, shucks" type of guy, and I didn't like it when actors played roles in real life. But tears came to Chris's eyes when she read the story. "Rob really got him," she said. "I can hear him saying that. He's got so much going for him, and yet he's so modest and unassuming. He doesn't seem to believe things could really go right for once."

"He could have fooled me."

"You saw him after a performance, when he was on a high. He's really a very sweet, rather insecure person."

"That's what Mickey says about Kruzick."

Chris touched her long nose with an equally long finger, a sure sign she was getting upset. "Listen, you don't have to—"

"I'm sorry. I liked the guy. Really. I just thought he laid it on a little thick in the interview."

"You don't know him." She went into her own office. I didn't know if he was Mr. Right or not, but I could see she was in deep.

* * *

Rob did a few more stories about the auction over the next few days, and we got four bidders. We set "The Great Sourdough Starter Auction," as *Chronicle* readers had come to know it, for noon the following Tuesday, at the modest offices of Nicholson and Schwartz. Monday night Peter had Chris and Rob and me over for dinner.

He had a two-room apartment in one of those shabby buildings that San Francisco is full of, the kind you hate going to because the hallway carpet stinks and no one ever seems to vacuum the stairs. Peter's had high ceilings and a fresh coat of high-gloss avocado-colored paint. His furniture was Cost Plus wicker, but he'd painted it aubergine and had had paisley cushions made for it. He'd ripped up the smelly carpet that probably came with the apartment, buffed the floor, and scattered tan and white cotton throw rugs about. A few nicely framed charcoal drawings hung on the walls.

It was a very eccentric, very elegant place, and it had obviously cost hardly anything. If I were starting to see Peter as a very resourceful young man, dinner persuaded me further. He served us homemade fettucine with homemade pesto, a salad of Belgian endive and watercress, and pineapple sherbet he'd made himself.

I thought maybe Chris was on to a good thing. The two of them had been together every spare minute since they'd met, so I guess she thought so, too.

The bidders had agreed to Rob's presence at the auction, and he was hoping to interview them afterward, but he wanted a little background information about them. That was the ostensible purpose of the dinner—to fill him in.

Rob got down to business after dinner. "So," he said, whipping out his notebook, "who are the bidders?"

Chris spoke before Peter had a chance. "Everybody who's anybody."

"Meaning?"

"Robert Tosi," said Peter.

"Of the Tosi Bakery? Wow." Rob was impressed for good reason. When the Martinelli company folded, the Tosi loaf had become the sourdough of choice. Most of the old restaurants served Tosi bread, though some of the newer, more chic ones bought their bread from one of the new, chic bakeries.

"Who else?" asked Rob.

"Tony Tosi."

"I don't get it. Are there two Tosi bakeries?"

"In a manner of speaking. Tony runs the Palermo Bakery." This was the oldest and best established of the new sourdough emporia.

"Are Tony and Bob related?"

"Brothers."

"You've got to be kidding."

"It's an even better story than you think. They're bitter rivals. Barely speak to each other."

"You know them?"

"I grew up with them. Their dad worked for my dad before he left to start his own bakery."

"This is great stuff."

"It gets better. The next bidder is a guy named Clayton Thompson."

"Who's he?"

"He was sent here from New York by none other than Conglomerate Foods—the frozen cake and pie folks. They want to market frozen sourdough."

"I've died and gone to heaven. The two local biggies, brother against brother, and a giant, man-eating, New York–based corporation."

If Chris could have looked like a cat or a cow, she would have. She had to make do with looking like what she was—a very contented Virginia aristocrat. Peter looked like a kid with a new bicycle.

"The fourth one's not so exciting," I said. "Some lady from Sonoma."

"Ah, a provincial upstart—and a lady, too. I hope she's photogenic."

Peter shrugged. "She's okay if you like short blondes." Chris has the delicate skin of a blonde, but her hair is a rich light brown, and she's six feet tall. So that was a tactful thing to say, and Peter reached for her hand as he said it.

"What's her name?" asked Rob.

"Sally Devereaux. Of the Plaza Bakery."

"Never heard of it. Anybody know anything about it?"

"The bread," said Peter, "is incredibly good."

"*Incredibly* good?"

"Fantastic."

"So what does she need the starter for?"

"Beats me. Why do any of them need it? I never have gotten the hang of any of this." He got up and came back with a tray of brandy snifters and a bottle of cognac. "I've been saving this," he said, and was handing drinks around when the doorbell rang.

He stopped what he was doing, walked over to the intercom, and asked who was there.

"Sally Devereaux," said the intercom. Peter pushed a button. He came back and finished pouring the drinks. "I guess," he said, "we can ask her right now why she wants the starter."

Sally Devereaux was not only blond; she was very pale. She was wearing jeans and a pink sweater that must have been an extra-large. It fit her snugly.

She was short, as Peter had said, rather plump, and rather top-heavy. Her hair was short and curly. A soft, fluffy kind of woman. And at the moment a very frightened one.

Tears started down her face when she saw Peter had company. "Oh, Peter, I'm so sorry. I didn't know—"

"It's all right." Awkwardly, he rubbed the back of her sweater. "It's okay." He made a gesture to Chris, and she poured Sally a brandy. "Sit down."

Sally did, and Peter made introductions. By that time Sally had a better hold on herself. "You're all here about the auction?"

We nodded.

"I just had a threatening phone call. Someone called and told me not to bid."

Rob leaned forward in his chair. Sometimes I thought he

had a funny way of looking at people—as if they were all
characters in one of his stories and not real at all. It worried
me. "A man or a woman?" he said.

Sally shuddered. "One of those whispery voices. Peter, I
can't do it, I can't do it. I just can't." Her voice rose on each
"can't."

"It's okay," said Chris. She waved at Sally's glass. "I
think the brandy might help." Sally sipped it, but she was
still very pale.

"What did the voice say?" asked Rob.

"It said, 'You know who this is. Drop out or you might
get hurt.' And then it hung up. I mean *he* hung up."

Rob was leaning even closer. "You know who it was,
then?"

"Of course." She looked at Peter. "It's them. It's got to
be. God knows what they'd do. They're used to it. They were
raised that way."

"Who?" asked Rob, but Peter waved him quiet.

"Sally," he said softly. "You're being ridiculous. I hope
you'll reconsider about the auction." He stood up, signaling
her to leave.

She stood, too, and took a step closer to Peter. "But—"

He put a hand on her shoulder. "I'm sure it's just some
nut. I hope to see you tomorrow."

He saw her to the door and patted her back as she left. The
whole thing seemed fishily perfunctory. If Peter were really
as good a guy as Chris thought, I figured he knew something
about Sally that the rest of us didn't.

He came back looking embarrassed. "This came up when
she called about the auction," he said. "She's got some crazy
idea about the—excuse me, I'd better get that."

Peter picked up the phone. "Mr. Thompson, how are
you?" He listened for a moment, reassured Thompson about
something, and hung up. "Clayton Thompson got a call,
too. He thinks it's the mob."

"Is that what Sally thought?" asked Rob.

"Not exactly. Sally's fears are a little more specific. I guess
I'd better tell you. She thinks if you're Italian, you're auto-

matically some kind of criminal.'' He shrugged. "It's crazy."

"You mean,'' said Rob, "she thinks it's one of the Tosis.''

"It's nuts.'' Peter was getting very upset. "I grew up with them. They're honest business people.''

"Peter,'' said Chris, "some nut might call one person, but two got calls. Somebody is trying to stop the auction.''

He shrugged again, looking frustrated.

Chris spoke slowly, as if she were afraid to: "It must be Anita."

Rob zeroed in: "Who's Anita?''

"My sister,'' Peter said. "The one who didn't inherit the starter."

Rob's face showed he didn't get it.

"She wanted it,'' said Peter. "And I wanted the house. But our parents didn't see it that way. She never gave up the idea of starting up the Martinelli Bakery again.''

"And,'' said Chris, "she's been begging him to call off the auction.''

"What difference does it make?'' Peter was practically shouting. "Anita's not going to hurt anybody. And neither are the Tosis. Everyone's getting hysterical for no reason.''

"I think,'' I said, "we should call the police.''

Peter picked up the phone and dialed. But he didn't call the cops. He said, "Bob? Peter Martinelli. I was just wondering—has anything odd happened tonight?''

After he finished talking, he turned to the rest of us. "Bob Tosi got a call and shrugged it off. Then his brother called and said he'd gotten one. Accused Bob of being the caller.''

"I really think—'' I said, but that was as far as I got.

"Look,'' said Peter. "Let's call it a night, okay? See you at noon.''

Chris looked hurt, and he gave her hair a reassuring ruffle. "Not you. You stick around.''

CHAPTER 3

Chris came in late the next morning, about ten, but I was with a client. In fact, both of us had a busy morning, so we didn't talk at all before the auction. Rob turned up at 11:45, and we went into Chris's office to help her arrange the chairs and make coffee—Kruzick had made some that morning, but it was too awful to serve. It wasn't quite twelve when he appeared at the door and said Clayton Thompson was there.

Thompson was a slight fellow, with thinning blond hair and a thick southern accent. He was from North Carolina and took a shine to Chris, whose own accent got a little thicker when she talked to him. Rob and I listened mostly, while they "passed the time of day," which, in their language, means "made polite conversation."

"How long you been in New York, Mr. Thompson?"

"Oh, seven, eight years. We were in Atlanta before that, my wife and I. Then the comp'ny said move, so we moved."

"Any kids?"

"Two boys. I just happen to have a couple of pictures if y'all'd be interested." Chris said we certainly would, and he showed us snaps of cute towheads.

There was something about him that was knotted up hard and very controlled beneath the easy manner. I couldn't put my finger on it, but I wondered if his job would be on the line if he didn't get the starter.

"Mr. Robert Tosi to see you," said Kruzick.

Tosi stepped into the room. He was dark, burly, and had

something I liked around the eyes, but I couldn't put my finger on that, either. He was dressed in khaki pants, a sports shirt with no tie, and an old corduroy jacket. I didn't much care for the outfit, as I felt it set a bad example for Kruzick, who tended to emulate Rob in his dress. Reporters, as you may know, always wear old corduroy jackets, and that's fine for them, but I feel a law office deserves more dignity. Kruzick does not share my opinion.

Despite his taste in clothes, Tosi had a warm handshake and a nice smile. He sat down, crossed his legs, and started chatting up Thompson.

"This your first trip?"

"Yes. It's a beautiful city."

"You should take a side trip to the wine country—breathe some fresh air for a change."

Thompson looked a bit sheepish. "I'm afraid I don't have much extra time."

"What have you seen so far?"

Thompson flushed. "Ah—not much. Nob Hill, and that's about it. I'm staying at the Stanford Court." He appeared at a loss for words. It was odd; he had seemed so courtly and comfortable a few minutes before.

But I thought Tosi's presence might have thrown him a bit off his stride. The man seemed to fill up a room, somehow. He had a sort of overflowing confidence that wasn't exactly intimidating—to me, anyway—but might have been off-putting to a man. Especially a man who was about to go up against him in a big business deal.

I wondered how much money was about to change hands. Chris didn't think half a million bucks was out of the question.

Kruzick brought Sally Devereaux in. She had on a beige suit and a light blue silk blouse with a bow. Her shoes were silly T-straps with four-inch heels. Her color had returned; in fact, her cheeks were quite attractively pink.

Tosi rose and stepped toward her, as if to kiss her. She stepped back and offered her hand.

"Sally. You're looking good."

She said, "Bob," and nodded.

He seemed to unhinge her a little, too. She turned quickly to Thompson and gave him a big smile.

"I've heard good things about your bakery," he said.

"It's only a couple of years old, but I'm hoping to expand. I think I really do have a good product."

"I'll have to try it sometime," said Tosi.

"You mean you haven't?" Sally sounded outraged.

He looked confused, as if he couldn't quite remember. "I really don't think I—"

"You don't even remember?"

He shrugged a pair of massive shoulders. "Sourdough tastes pretty much like sourdough."

Sally didn't answer. She was fuming.

Tony Tosi came in. He was big, like his brother, and they both had the same square jawline, but Tony's hair was thinning faster and he seemed less substantial. I wasn't sure what the difference was, but I figured maybe Bob worked out and Tony didn't. They had different styles of dress as well. Tony was wearing a suit and every kind of Gucci accessory on the market.

"Bob," said Tony. "Sally."

He made no move to shake hands with either of the people he spoke to, and sat down quickly so he wouldn't have to shake with Thompson either.

Chris looked at her watch. It was ten after twelve. "I'm sure Mr. Martinelli will be here soon," she said. "Would anyone like coffee?"

They all said yes and not much else. It was true they were adversaries, but they were also experienced business people, and they were doing precious little to keep up minimum standards of politeness. At first I put it down to the feud between the brothers, but it wasn't only that. Sally had snapped at Bob and generally seemed out of sorts. Thompson was uneasy about something. Perhaps they were thinking about the threatening phone calls. Maybe they were sitting there trying to figure out which of the other three had made them.

"Excuse me," said Chris, and went to my office. When she came back, she said, "I just called Mr. Martinelli and got no answer. So I'm sure he's on his way."

"It's twelve-twenty," said Sally. "You'd think he could be on time for his own auction."

"Miss Nicholson," said Tony, "I think if he isn't here by twelve-thirty, we have to assume he isn't serious about selling the starter."

Chris looked as if she might cry.

"Mr. Tosi," I said, "you may assume anything you want. When Mr. Martinelli arrives, the auction will take place."

Rob gave me an "atta-girl" look. I could tell he was feeling sorry for Chris.

We gave them more coffee and even offered drinks, but no one accepted. Rob and Thompson and Bob Tosi and I managed to keep up a little desultory conversation, but Chris couldn't say a word, and Sally and Tony appeared to have taken vows of silence.

At 12:45, Bob Tosi stretched, looked at his watch, and said he had a lunch date. "I expect the rest of you do, too," he said. "Why don't we leave together and set another date for the auction? I'm sure Mr. Martinelli must have gotten tied up or he'd have been here by now."

"May as well," said Thompson, rising and straightening his tie.

Tony rose without a word.

Only Sally seemed reluctant. She continued to sit a bit longer, looking as if she were trying to think of something to say. After a moment, she got up and left with the others.

Chris was dialing Peter's number before they were out the door. She put down the receiver, sighing. "No answer."

"Look," I said, "I'll go out and get sandwiches." She nodded.

"I'll go with you," said Rob. It was obvious Chris needed to be alone.

We came back with three pastramis on rye and three Cokes. Rob ate all of his, I managed half of mine, and Chris stared into space while we ate. Every now and then she'd pick up half her sandwich and stare at it instead of the horizon, but she never got as far as biting into it.

She called Peter's again. No answer. "I'm going over there."

"Chris, you can't—"

"Rebecca, this is no time to be cool."

Rob looked baffled, but I had to give Chris credit. She'd put her finger on the very thing I was thinking—when your boyfriend stands you up, you shouldn't go spying on him or he might get the idea you like him. Maybe I'd never grow up.

"I guess not," I said. "I think we should all go."

She didn't protest.

Peter didn't answer his doorbell, and the manager didn't answer hers. But just as we were about to give up, a woman who recognized Chris came in from walking her dog and let us in. We climbed the two flights of smelly stairs to Peter's apartment and knocked. He didn't answer. Chris tried the door—and jumped back when it opened.

Rob pushed it wide enough to see what police call "signs of a struggle." A lamp was knocked over, and one of Peter's charcoal drawings hung askew, as if someone had fallen against the wall. The furniture was like that, too—sort of pushed around and out of place. Peter was sitting on the couch, staring at us. He was wearing a white terrycloth robe with a number of bulletholes in it. Peter's blood had run out of his chest and turned the robe a nasty rust color.

If I'd been alone, I'd have closed the door and run like crazy, but Chris is made of sterner stuff. She yelled Peter's name and ran over to him. She touched him on both shoulders, as if to embrace him. His body fell forward.

It fell against Chris. She recoiled and swayed. Rob rushed forward, held her, maneuvered her into a chair. I stepped into the room and stared at Chris and Rob, not looking at Peter's body and not knowing what to do. I thought I should call the police, but I was worried about messing up fingerprints. It's funny what you think about at a time like that.

"Stay with her," said Rob, already headed toward the

bedroom. He came back in a minute. "There's no one here. And no gun. I'll call the cops."

"Use your handkerchief."

"Huh?"

"Fingerprints."

He looked at me as if I were nuts, picked up the receiver with his bare hands, and in a moment asked for Inspector Martinez, a homicide cop we'd met a year or so earlier.

"Rebecca," said Chris. "I think I'd better lie down."

She was awfully pale. "Put your head on your lap." She sat doubled over for a moment, and then I heard her start to sob. I figured she couldn't faint if she had the strength to cry, so I got a pillow and put it on the floor. She lay down while I went to get her some of Peter's brandy. It was a few minutes before she could sip it.

Peter's body was lying sideways on the sofa now. None of us wanted to look at it, but we were afraid to cover it up.

Rob looked at me sheepishly. "I've got to call city desk."

"No. They'll send a photographer."

He nodded, easily persuaded. I knew him well enough to figure out what was in his mind. Technically, he wasn't really doing his job if he didn't call for a camera, but he didn't want to look at his paper the next morning and see a picture of Peter's covered-up body being carried to a coroner's wagon. Any more than I did. And neither one of us wanted Chris to see it.

We heard sirens, then clomping on the stairs, and then some uniformed cops came in. One of them took us downstairs to wait for the homicide inspectors.

It didn't take Martinez very long. He was accompanied, as usual, by his partner, Curry, who always seemed to keep quiet while Martinez blustered. Both of them wore rumpled brown suits, as usual, and Martinez had on a blue tie with little pigs all over it. It was probably meant to be funny, but it suited him. He had wispy dark hair and a pale, washed-out face that always wore an impatient look, as if he wished you would just shut up. And yet he kept asking you questions and more questions and complaining that you weren't telling him enough. As for Curry, he had no visible moles, scars, or other distinguishing marks, so it's hard to describe him. But I'll try: He had plain features, brownish hair, and ordinary eyes. He must have been great at undercover work—no one alive could remember a face like that.

Neither of them liked me much either.

Rob explained the situation, and they went upstairs and came down again. Martinez spoke to Chris: "What happened, Miss Nicholson?"

"Didn't Rob tell you?"

"He told us he left you with Martinelli last night. Did you spend the night with the victim?"

"I don't think that's any of your business."

"Let's put it this way. Did you kill him?"

"How dare you!" She was taller than he was, and standing very straight.

He waved a placating hand. "It's my business to know when you last saw him alive."

"I left at nine this morning. He said he had a ten o'clock appointment."

"Who with?"

"That was none of *my* business."

"So who was it?"

"I told you I didn't know."

"Well, next time say it a little clearer."

"I don't have to talk to you."

"Where was his appointment—here or somewhere else?"

"He didn't say."

"Okay. Do you know who his next of kin is?"

"His parents are dead. He has a sister—Anita Ashton."

They talked a few minutes more, but I didn't listen. I was thinking of Anita Ashton—I'd known her for quite a while.

CHAPTER 4

Chris and I went back to the office, leaving Rob to get his story. We sent Kruzick home, after having him cancel the rest of the day's appointments. Then Chris found a bottle of bourbon and made herself a drink. I declined—I think you have to be from Virginia to stand the stuff.

For a while she stared out the window, and I let her. When she was ready to talk, she said, "I'm going to find the sucker who did this."

I nodded.

"Will you help me?" she asked.

"Sure." Revenge may not be the most uplifting theme of the human psyche, but it can be comforting sometimes. Of course I was going to help her.

"There's something I didn't tell Martinez. Peter got a phone call sometime last night. He took it in the living room and talked a long time. He didn't mention till this morning that he had an appointment at ten."

"You think the caller made the appointment?"

"Yes. And kept it and murdered him."

I nodded again. It sounded right to me. All we had to do was find out who it was.

The phone rang. Chris reached for it automatically. "Chris Nicholson. Yes, I'm his lawyer, but—oh. Mrs. Ashton. I have no idea whether he left a will or not. I was representing him on another matter. Yes . . . may I ask why you want to know? Very well. It's at Fail-Safe Cryogenics. They're listed in the phone book."

23

"Let me guess," I said. "Peter's sister think she's inherited the starter."

"You got it. She wants to go and look at it."

"Weird."

She shrugged. "Understandable, I guess. She's wanted it for years."

"Why didn't she just offer to buy it from him?"

"He offered to trade it for the house, but she wouldn't go for it. Seemed to think he couldn't be trusted with a chunk of money of any size. He got mad and they had a fight. He swore he'd see she never got it. Years later, when he was really broke, she did offer to buy it—for $5,000. Can you imagine that? Tried to pull a fast one on her own brother."

"It doesn't surprise me. I know her."

"You know Anita Ashton?"

"I took her course a few years ago. Do you know who she is?"

"Sure. She's an internationally known time-management consultant. Her book was on the best-seller list for seventeen months or something. Celebrity clients up and down the state. Movie stars, execs, you name it."

"Not to mention Rebecca Schwartz, Jewish feminist lawyer. She's kind of a hard case, Chris. But likable—you know the type? Underneath the first steely layer, she's sort of vulnerable. But she's so worried somebody's going to take advantage of her, she tries to do it to them first."

Chris sighed. "I guess that's how you get rich."

"Tell me something. Was Peter ever married?"

"No. He was forty-one and never even engaged."

"In that case, assuming he didn't make a will, there probably isn't anyone else to inherit the starter. That gives Anita an excellent murder motive."

Chris looked excited. "She must have made the threatening phone calls. Maybe she tried to stop the auction and it didn't work, so she killed him."

"Let's not overlook anything. Maybe one of the bidders

made the phone calls to get everyone else to withdraw. Then when it didn't work, that person killed him.''

"At any rate, he must have been killed to stop the auction.''

"Well, for now Anita's the best suspect. It couldn't hurt to go down to City Hall and look at the Martinelli will.''

"Okay.'' She perked up at the prospect of doing something.

We walked down to the Montgomery Street BART station (that's Bay Area Rapid Transit) and took the train two stops to Civic Center. The station's a block or two from City Hall, and the whole area is full of wind tunnels blowing close to the buildings. It was February, and that meant they were fierce. So we walked across Civic Center Plaza, which was sunny and pleasant.

City Hall is an old-fashioned gray stone building, trimmed here and there in blue and gold. When you walk in, you're standing in a wonderful rotunda in front of a sweeping stairway. Unfortunately, the effect is ruined by the presence of a guard who makes you walk through an unsightly metal detector.

We took the elevator to the clerk's office on the third floor. It's a place of musty ledgers rather than crisp microfiches, a picturesque anachronism in the computer age. The people who work there, many of them elderly ladies, are friendly and unhurried. I always enjoy going there.

We found the Martinelli will without any trouble. It was exactly as Peter had said: The house had been left to Anita; the starter to Peter. There were no provisions for the disposition of the estate in the event that either of the younger Martinellis died. In other words, Peter was free to leave the starter to whomever he chose. If he hadn't made a will, it looked as if it would go to his closest relative—his sister, Anita. So that was that.

"What,'' said Chris, "do we do now?''

"I can't think of anything. If Anita did it, I'm sure the cops will figure it out.''

She looked very downcast.

"Let's go to my house for dinner."

"It's only four o'clock."

"So go home and change." I reached out and touched her arm. "Look, Chris, there's nothing else we can do right now, except maybe have our own private wake for Peter."

She nodded. I could see tears in her eyes. I figured she'd have a good cry while she was home.

We went back to the office, got our cars, and I drove my old gray Volvo to Fisherman's Wharf to pick up a couple of Dungeness crabs. Chris wouldn't be able to eat much, and I figured cracked crab, which gives you a lot to do with your hands, ought to be about right. I got a loaf of Bob Tosi's sourdough to go with it, and a jug of white wine. Then I headed toward my apartment on Telegraph Hill.

I was glad, as always, to be home. My apartment is white and red mostly; it cheers me up. Besides, I don't live alone. I have so many pets I can't even count them. They live in a hundred-gallon saltwater aquarium. I've got fish, shrimp, sea anemones, sea snails, and at the moment, a sea horse. I say at the moment because he wasn't the first one I'd had—I can't seem to get them to live very long, but I keep trying because they're so cute. This one's name was Durango.

I fed Durango and his friends, and then I showered and changed into jeans. There was plenty of time left and no dinner to cook, so I played the piano awhile, Vivaldi to cheer me up. I like something baroque at the end of a long hard day.

Chris turned up around six-thirty, rosy and refreshed. She had on jeans—skinny ones with about a forty-inch inseam. She is one long, tall drink of water.

"You look a lot better."

"I went jogging."

Of course she had. I felt momentarily guilty. If I jogged, maybe my legs would get skinnier, but it was no good wishing they'd get longer. I am a five-feet-five endomorph who does well to get in a little tennis now and then. The sight of Chris can make me envious and guilty and admiring all at once. At the moment, since she looked as if she might pull through, it made me happy.

"I'll get us some wine. You put on a record."

She picked some noncommittal jazz, neither happy nor sad. When we were facing each other, her eyes overflowed. "I'm going to miss him."

"I know you are. I wish—"

I was going to say I wished I knew something comforting to say, but the phone rang.

"Rebecca, it's your mother. I've just heard the news. On TV, I had to hear it."

"We're okay, Mom. Chris is here and everything's fine. I'm sorry I forgot to call you."

"It's nothing, darling. Your father had to go and lie down, that's all."

"Oh, come on, Mom. It takes more than that to upset Dad."

"Rebecca, answer me something, will you? Why must you always get involved with people who kill each other?"

"Mom, please. Peter was Chris's boyfriend. Your very own younger daughter's paramour, Alan Kruzick, introduced them. Blame it on Kruzick for a change."

"It's not Alan's fault, darling. You're the one who found the body."

"Believe me, Mom, I wouldn't have if I could have helped it."

"Just tell me, Rebecca. Why must you go on doing this sort of thing? You're nearly thirty years old."

"Mom, I'll tell you what. I'm going to stop it right now. I'm never finding another dead body, and that's final. I'm changing my ways and I owe it all to you."

"That's right, make fun of your mother."

"Mom, I didn't mean it that way. Honest. Can I talk to Dad a minute?"

"No, dear. He's gone out for ice cream. He overeats when he's worried."

"Oh, poor Daddy. Tell him I'm sorry, okay? I have company so I'd better go now."

"Give Chris our love. Poor baby, losing a boyfriend like that."

" 'Bye, Mom."

I let out a yell of frustration, but Mom's good for Chris. She was laughing her head off.

"My mom said to give you her love. Apparently, I've been a bad girl for finding Peter's body, but you're a poor baby."

"Your mom's a riot."

Mom didn't amuse me at the moment. "I'm glad you're feeling better," I snapped, and started melting butter to dip the crab into. Chris got out the crab and arranged it on plates.

"I wish I could have another chance," Chris said.

"With Peter?"

She nodded.

"It's only natural to feel that way."

We sat down, and Chris picked at her crab while I made quick work of mine.

"I know he liked me a lot," she said, "but . . ."

She couldn't finish her sentence. I didn't know if it would help or not, but I blurted out what I felt: "Listen, Chris. Here's what I think about Peter. A man his age who'd never been married probably wasn't about to change his ways."

"What makes you think I want to get married?"

"Sometimes you say you do. Then again, sometimes you say you don't. So sometimes I think one thing and sometimes the other."

"I wasn't thinking about marrying Peter. Yet, I mean. I just wish we'd had a little more time to—I don't know—understand each other."

"Something's bothering you, isn't it?"

She started crying again. "He's dead!"

"I'm sorry. I meant something was already bothering you—when he was alive."

She looked very unhappy. "He was a little . . . distant."

"You mean cold? Sexually cold?"

She nodded, sobbing. "It wasn't only that—he was so

hard to get to know; if we'd had more time, I might have—''

"Oh, Chris, it wasn't your fault. All the time in the world probably wouldn't have made a difference."

"You don't think so?"

"No. Some guys are just like that."

"You really think it wasn't me?"

"Of course not."

"You're so lucky to have Rob!"

I was lucky to have Rob and I knew it. He had a million good qualities I could have enumerated, but Chris was feeling sorry for herself, so I belittled my own good fortune, zeroing in on the one thing about Rob that bothered me. "He's not perfect, you know. Being a newspaper reporter is an odd job. Every now and then he gets his priorities mixed up and his stories get to be more important than real life."

"Really? But we're all very involved with our work."

"This is different. Reporters aren't like you and me. On the other hand, he's always around when I need him. He doesn't nag me, and he doesn't press me to do things I don't want to do. And he doesn't have to be babied."

Chris smiled. "Any more like him at home?"

"Thank God! The fever's broken. You're going to live, aren't you?"

"I'm probably going to have a few bad days, but that's okay. Knowing Peter was worth it. I just wish he'd had the chance to get over what was bothering him. I don't think he really felt loveable; I think that's why he was so alone."

Rob called then. "How's Chris?"

"Better. She thinks if she can't have Peter, someone like you might do."

"Little does she know."

"That's what I told her. Thanks for calling—it was sweet of you."

"Wait. There's a development. Peter's sister went over to Fail-Safe Cryogenics to look at her inheritance."

"I know. She called Chris to find out where it was."

"When she got there, she didn't mention Peter was dead. Just said she was his sister and asked to have a gander."

"And they showed it to her?"

"They tried. It seems there was a technical difficulty."

"Come on. I'm on the edge of my chair."

"The starter wasn't there."

CHAPTER
5

Sometime—who knew when?—the starter had apparently been stolen. Whether before or after the murder was anybody's guess. Or whether this year or last year. The starter had been freeze-dried very fast, in small pellets, in a vacuum—that was the only way you could be sure of keeping both microorganisms alive. It was stored in little vials in a chest freezer charged with liquid nitrogen to keep it extra cold. Anyone could have taken it out in a liquid-nitrogen vacuum bottle, the type used for transporting bull sperm. These, Rob explained, were aluminum and stainless steel containers about the size of large thermos bottles. You could keep the starter frozen indefinitely as long as you kept the thermos charged with liquid nitrogen. So maybe someone had taken it recently, and maybe not.

As for Anita, she'd become the number-one suspect in Peter's murder. Rob said the cops were still talking to her but hadn't booked her yet. He figured they probably would, sometime that night, and the *Examiner*, the afternoon rag, would get the story first. He was pretty mad about that. It was one insult right on top of another, because it was already too late for the *Chron* to get the missing starter story in Wednesday's paper. That meant that was the *Ex*'s story, for sure, even if the cops let Anita go. But they wouldn't, said Rob, not in a million years. Airtight case, he said. Some cop buddy had told him so.

Next morning, about ten-thirty or so, I raced out to get the first edition of the *Ex*. I was surprised they were playing the missing starter story below the fold—I guess they'd decided it was a *Chron* extravaganza, a bit beneath their dignity. I scanned the story quickly, looking for news of Anita. But there wasn't any.

I called Rob for late-breaking details. She'd been released.

It was this way. A divorced lady, she'd spent Monday night at her house with her long-term lover. He'd driven her to her offices. At about nine-thirty, just as they were leaving, a neighbor came over to borrow something. The boyfriend dropped her off to teach a class at ten o'clock. Since she lived in San Anselmo, across the Golden Gate Bridge, there was no time for her to have killed Peter between nine-thirty and ten. Even if the boyfriend were lying for her, she had other witnesses to support her at both ends of the half hour.

Much as I hated to admit it, it looked as if she were innocent. Chris was in court, so I took matters into my own hands. I phoned Anita, wondering whether she'd remember me.

She did. "Rebecca Schwartz. Have you licked it yet?"

"Have I licked what?"

"Procrastination. You're a terrible procrastinator."

"No, I'm not. I mean—I guess I have licked it." I hadn't procrastinated in so long, I hardly remembered doing it— Anita's course had done me a lot of good.

"Good work. What can I do for you?"

"I'm Chris Nicholson's partner."

"Oh, you're that Schwartz."

"I need to talk to you."

"Let's see. . . ." I could almost see Anita consulting her digital watch. "It's eleven-thirty now and I was planning to play tennis at lunch—I was hoping to pick up a partner, but you'll do. That is, if you play. Do you?"

"Am I from Marin County?"

"Good. Noon at the Golden Gateway Tennis Club." She spoke so briskly that a person who didn't know her could get the idea she was being rude. But she wasn't—she just didn't have any time to waste. Of course Anita would play tennis at lunchtime. Of course she'd belong to the Golden Gateway club—which was close to her office—instead of the San Francisco Tennis Club, which was south of Market. And of course she'd combine tennis, lunch, and a talk with a lawyer about her dead brother. She hadn't gotten where she was by wasting time.

I just had time to go home, get into my tennis togs, and get over there. I wasn't going to like playing on an empty stomach, but then Peter Martinelli probably didn't like being dead.

I was glad I'd dressed at home. Anita was already warming up. She had a good figure, skinny for an Italian. Her bones were not so fine as Peter's, and she had rather an ordinary, darkish face. But her thirty-dollar haircut made the best of it. It also revealed a tightness in her jaw that wasn't sexy but probably worked to her advantage in business. She looked slightly intimidating—very much the crisp, no-nonsense businesswoman.

She consulted her watch. "You're two minutes late."

"Mea culpa."

"No, that's not bad. It's okay, really. I always allow for the other guy being five minutes late. Have you ever noticed how few people are punctual?"

"Often, ever since I took your course."

"You're a good student. Want to warm up?"

I shook my head. "Let's just play."

She had a strong serve and terrific focus. Her small brown eyes were everywhere at once. Oddly, her hair seemed not to move as she whipped around the court, even after it was dripping from perspiration. Which it was after about ten minutes. Mine was, too. We were almost well matched—at any rate, I was able to keep her moving, a good trick with my stomach growling the way it was. But I couldn't win. Each game was a struggle, going in and out of advantage, but the final point was always hers. We played two sets and I didn't win once.

In the sauna afterward, she asked again what she could do for me.

"Background," I said, "I guess. My partner and your brother were lovers."

"I thought so, but I wasn't sure. Especially when she turned out to be female."

"Peter was gay?"

She shrugged her naked shoulders. "I don't know, really. I guess not if he was seeing your partner."

"Let me go over this again. You don't know whether your own brother was gay or not?"

"I didn't see him much." She was silent for a bit. "He had women friends, yes. It was just an idea I had—that he might be bi. Didn't it occur to you?"

"It did, come to think of it."

"Well, if you want to know for sure, I can't help you."

"You don't seem very broken up about his death."

"Why should I be?" She stepped into the shower and turned it on, spritzing the fancy hairdo, then working shampoo in. "I hated him. I've hated him ever since I can remember. Whoever killed him did me a good turn."

"Why did you hate him so much?"

"Rebecca, did your family encourage you to become a lawyer?"

"Not exactly. They wanted me to be a doctor."

She laughed, and the sound was rather nasty. "You can't identify with me at all, can you? You have no idea what I was up against."

"I don't really see what you're saying."

"I haven't said it yet." She washed the soap out of her hair. "Would you say I have business sense?"

"No more than, say, the president of IBM does. How many mil' are you worth, anyhow?"

She looked right at me, and I noticed how small her eyes were—that hairdo really did wonders. "Several," she said. "And I made every penny without the slightest encouragement from my warm, loving Italian relatives."

"But Peter was poor—how could he have helped you?"

"By not existing, that's how!" She spoke venomously. "It's true what he told that reporter—he's got about as much of a head for business''—she looked around—''as that bar of soap.'' She kicked it and it skidded across the tiled floor. ''But just because he had a wing-wang, and I didn't, he got the starter.''

''Wing-wang?'' I was feeling a little lost. Also, I was starving.

''Because he was a boy, dammit! Let's go.''

I followed her out to the anteroom and lay down on one of the benches. She rang for a hair dryer and began reshaping the sculptured cut, using her comb viciously, as if she were angry at her own hair. ''You don't know anything about Italian families, do you?''

''Maybe Jewish families aren't that different. But I don't have any brothers.''

''Well, be glad of it—I'll bet you'd have wound up a social worker if you did.''

''My sister—'' I began, but she interrupted.

''I could never get my parents to see what I was, do you understand that? I guess Peter had the same problem, only in reverse, but that wasn't my concern. I had my own troubles. I wanted to be appreciated for being who I am, smart like Anita, not cute and flirty like someone I wasn't. It was wrong. It was unfair.''

''I get the idea you resented it.''

''Resent! I would have killed—'' She stopped in midsentence. Oddly, she let the hair dryer drop and her voice shook. ''I *didn't* kill him. I thought there was nothing I wanted more than to get that starter and start up the Martinelli Bakery again.'' She seemed not to believe her own words but to be trying them out to see if they fit. ''But now, I don't know. . . .''

''You don't know what?''

''I think I miss Peter. I think I'm sorry he's dead.''

''I thought you were glad.''

''I am, but I'm not, too—does that make sense?''

''It's a little complex.'' I started to get dressed.

''I really hated him, you know that? I wanted to humiliate him the way my parents always humiliated me—I wanted to show him up as incompetent. So you know what I did? I let it get in my way. If I'd offered him decent money for the starter, he'd have sold it to me and we'd both have been happy, but I had to control him into the bargain.''

"Peter mentioned something to that effect.''

"I *hated* him, Rebecca. But now I'm starting to feel funny inside, sort of empty, like I've lost something important.''

"Well, you have lost the starter.''

She smiled, apparently relieved at having some subject besides Peter to occupy her. "Maybe that's it. Incidentally, why do you want to know all this?''

"I'm looking for anything that might help find the murderer. The real question is why you've been so free to talk to me about it—I'm only a former student, after all.''

"Yes, but you showed great promise. Besides, I needed a tennis partner.''

"You could have picked one up.''

"Okay. I needed someone to talk to, I guess. I was feeling odd and not sure why. I wanted to talk to someone who was almost a stranger; otherwise I'd be making myself too vulnerable.''

"Even to your boyfriend?''

She nodded. "I'm a very clamped-down person. I want to thank you for this.''

And she actually shook my hand, in gratitude for letting me ask a lot of impertinent questions.

While I went home and changed back into my gray suit and silk blouse, I tried to figure her out. She was right about one thing—she *was* a very clamped-down person. Maybe too clamped-down to be having a sudden change of heart about a brother she'd hated for thirty-odd years.

On the other hand, it's only human to change your mind about someone who's dead; she could have killed him and then started to miss him. Except that she had an airtight alibi.

CHAPTER 6

After two sets of tennis and a sauna, I felt healthy enough for three people and hungry enough for a dozen. I had no qualms at all about scarfing down an entire frozen pizza before hitting Montgomery Street again.

"I know," said Kruzick when I went in. "What a dump, right? Listen, you want a lawyer with a fancy office, see Mel Belli, okay? Don't complain to me—I only work here."

"Alan, I'm warning you—I can get a Kelly girl."

"You may go in now, dear. Miss Nicholson's expecting you."

"Maybe not a Kelly girl—maybe a tommy gun." I whipped past his desk as I said that, with a rustle of skirts and a click of heels. Then I gave him a withering look over my shoulder. But he was already typing, the picture of serenity, as if his conscience were clear as a mountain stream. I was afraid I'd kill him one day—sooner rather than later, probably. But, remembering I had a question for him, I put it off for a few days. "Esteemed employee," I said.

"Yes, ma'am, Miss Schwartz, ma'am."

"That's more like it. Was Peter gay?"

"What do you mean? He was taking Chris out, wasn't he? Didn't they . . . you know. . . ." He made a two-fingered circle and put another finger through it.

"Alan, you're disgusting!"

"Hey, everybody does it—you ought to try it sometime."

"What I meant was, was there any gossip about Peter at the theater? Like there was about Nick Dresser, remember?

37

The one who was married to a lady named Carla but always turning up with a cute boy named Bob.''

"Oh, Nick. He was bi, no question about it. Once he asked if Mickey and I wanted to—"

"Alan! What about Peter?"

He was silent for a minute, thinking about it. Then he shrugged. "I don't know. It doesn't seem out of the question, does it? But I always thought he was just a loner."

"He didn't go out with women much?"

"Hardly ever. Hey, I think I see what you're getting at— you think he had a gay lover, huh? And the guy got jealous of Chris and perpetrated a crime of passion. That's it, isn't it?"

"Don't be ridiculous." Once again I whipped past him, doing a fair imitation of an imperious boss putting an upstart in his place.

"Hey, employer."

"What is it now?"

"There's something fishy about that starter theft. I think the cryogenics firm might be up to something."

I sighed. "And what, pray tell?"

"Well, look. If you're going to pay a bunch of money to have your starter frozen, shouldn't there be some guarantee? I mean, what if the warehouse burned down or something?"

"You'd be out of luck." I started walking toward Chris's office.

"Rebecca, listen to me a minute."

He sounded so serious, for once, that I did.

"A firm like that ought to have a control."

"A control?" I was beginning to see what he was getting at. "You mean, not one but two frozen starters—in two different places?"

"Go to the head of the class." And he went back to typing.

Chris came out of her office. "Did I hear what I think I did?"

Alan smirked. "Hee-hee. Idiot-child only one with

smarts." He scratched his armpit and made gorilla noises. Chris and I retreated.

"What," asked Chris, "is Pigball's name again? I've forgotten."

"Fail-Safe," I said, understanding instantly. Chris used made-up words when she couldn't remember real ones—which was often. Fortunately, her memory never seemed to fail her in court, but her close friends had to be good at interpreting.

She swung a phone book over to her side of the desk, turned to *F*, and dialed the cryogenics firm. The manager, apparently, was a *Chronicle* reader. From what I could gather, he was very sorry Chris had lost her client but awfully hungry for details of the murder. Chris gave him a few and then reeled in her reward.

"I understand the starter has been stolen . . . I was wondering about a control . . . Ah. I see." A couple of other questions, then good-bye.

When she hung up, the spark had returned to her eyes for the first time since Peter's death. "There *is* a control. Apparently, the underling who helped Anita didn't know about it. Panicked when he discovered the loss. The manager, having heard that Anita is not being held for murder, has been trying to get her to tell her. It seems he was out of town, only got back a few hours ago, and couldn't be sorrier for the inconvenience. If *he'd* been there, it certainly wouldn't have happened."

"Where's the control? In San Francisco or somewhere else?"

"He wouldn't say. I don't really blame him, do you?"

"I guess not. I just got back from playing tennis with Anita. I expect that's why he couldn't get her. It seems she hated Peter, but now she misses him, and even though she's glad he's dead, she's sort of sorry."

"How disappointing. She's supposed to be the sort of woman who knows her own mind."

"There's more."

"I can't say I'm thrilled about your tone of voice."

"It's not pretty."

"I'm sitting down, okay?"

"She'd already guessed you and Peter were lovers, but before she talked to you, she thought you might be a man."

Chris stared, unbelieving. "Peter was bi?"

"It's not that bad. Anita doesn't really know; she just had a feeling."

"Oh, God, I should have had the same feeling! What was I thinking of?"

"What do you mean?"

"He just—I don't know. He wasn't that interested in sex."

I breathed a little sigh of relief, glad that was all. "I guess lots of guys are like that."

"*I* guess I better get tested."

"Didn't you—uh—"

"Use condoms? Yes." She shrugged. "Last I heard they weren't foolproof."

"Well, I did ask Kruzick for the gossip on him. I'm happy to say there wasn't any. He apparently didn't truck with comely young men and was hardly ever seen with a woman."

"That's comforting."

"The only thing is—"

"I know. Maybe he had a gay lover and maybe we'll run into him. You know what I'm going to do about that? Pretend I'm Scarlett and think about it tomorrow." Her smile was looking a little too brave.

"You okay?"

"I can take it, Schwartzie."

"Don't call me Schwartzie. Or I won't tell you my idea."

"Yes, you will, if you've got one. What is it?"

"I think we have a professional duty to perform, as Peter's attorneys. Inasmuch as four people came to our offices expecting to bid on a sourdough starter, and inasmuch as we were in charge of that ill-fated auction, I think it's up to us to keep the four people up to date."

"Go on."

"They probably all read the *Examiner* and therefore think

the starter's been stolen. When actually another batch exists."

"You think Anita might still want to sell it?"

"Not a chance."

"Oh. Then wouldn't it be unethical to get their hopes up?"

"It certainly would. We wouldn't dream of doing such a thing. But, if there *is* a starter and they don't know about it, they can hardly make her an offer, can they? After all, we can't read her mind—maybe if the price were right, she *would* sell."

"I don't know, Rebecca. It doesn't really sound like any of our business."

"But what if one of them found out about it and the other three didn't? That person would have a very unfair advantage, don't you think?"

"Peter wouldn't have liked that."

"And we were his lawyers. So I think we ought to tell them as our last duty as his attorneys."

"How come you look so much like a little kid who's up to something?"

"Because I am, of course. We're going to pump them, and they're not even going to notice."

"You think *that's* ethical?"

"Certainly. We've agreed that it's our duty to tell them about the second starter. If we do it face to face instead of on the phone, that makes us even more conscientious. And if they want to get anything off their chests, we'll just be good guys and listen."

"Gosh, we're wonderful."

CHAPTER 7

I checked my watch. "Nearly three o'clock. We might be able to catch the Tosi boys at work."

Chris was already busy with a phone book. "Well, we can't catch both of them unless we work fast. One's in Colma and the other's in Oakland."

"Oakland? San Francisco sourdough is made in Oakland?"

"If you ask me, it beats Colma." We both laughed. Oakland, across the bay to the east, is the butt of a million San Francisco jokes, but Colma, a little way down the peninsula, is a necropolis. If there were a bakery there, that meant the town wasn't all cemeteries, but that would be news to most people. It certainly was to Chris and me.

"But Colma's closer," I said. "Which one's there?"

"Tosi. I mean the Tosi Bakery. Bob."

"Let's go."

It was no trouble finding the Tosi Bakery—anything above ground in Colma sticks out like a pimple. The guard at the door rang Bob Tosi to ask if he'd see us, and apparently he said he would. We were issued name tags and waved on.

Bob Tosi was better looking than I'd remembered him. I'd liked something around his eyes and I still liked it. I still liked his nice smile. His casual clothes somehow looked better in Colma than they had on Montgomery Street. I forgave him for them and glanced at the fourth finger of his left hand. No ring. He wasn't my type, exactly, but he was at-

42

tractive enough and he was rich. What was he doing on the loose? I wondered.

The man exuded confidence. So did his office, though it wasn't "tasteful"—at least, it wasn't an all-of-a-piece, interior-designed, tan-and-orange wonder, like most people's offices. It had a worn green carpet on the floor, bits of Naugahyde furniture here and there, and original paintings on the walls. Good ones. A dark green and yellow one of two swimmers caught my eye. "That's a Mary Robertson, isn't it?"

Tosi looked surprised. "You're an art buff?"

Really, how annoying. I said what was on my mind: "You can like art without being a 'buff,' whatever that is."

Chris tried to hide a smile, but she needn't have bothered. "Touché," said Tosi, and laughed heartily. "I've just started collecting in the last couple of years. I guess I don't really know much. Do you think Mary Robertson's good?"

"Certainly. Everyone does."

"And you, Chris?"

"You don't really care what I think, do you?"

"Not in the least." He put his feet up on his desk. "Now what can I do for you?"

"We came," said Chris, "because we have some good news for you. The starter's been found."

"The starter's . . ." He slapped his hand to his forehead, as if he'd forgotten something. "Oh, yes, Peter's starter. But I don't understand."

"They had another batch."

He nodded. "Of course. They would."

"So that's our good news. It may come back on the market after all, though we don't really think Anita will sell it. We thought we'd better tell all the bidders, just in case."

"I see. You mean there might be an auction after all?"

"I doubt it. We just thought we should let you know the starter exists."

"That's nice of you." He looked at me, then at Chris, who looked miserable. "But I don't think I care much. It's just a PR gimmick, really. The Tosi Bakery doesn't need it."

"But—"

He held up a hand. "I've done some thinking since Peter died. About why he was killed."

"We've done a lot of thinking about it."

"Peter wasn't the type to get involved in romantic triangles," he said.

I winced and avoided looking at Chris. She said nothing.

"And if it wasn't that, what's left? I think someone wanted that auction stopped. Otherwise, why the threatening phone calls?"

"Feelings were running kind of high," said Chris.

"And over a thing that's just a gimmick—for Conglomerate especially. Thank God I don't have to deal with that kind of garbage."

"What kind of garbage?" I asked.

"Working for a big company that's all image and no substance. They need that starter. I mean, who are they trying to kid? Nationally distributed frozen sourdough!"

"I don't follow you."

"It's going to be second-rate, no matter what. Good sourdough is sourdough that's baked today. So Conglomerate needs a gimmick." He looked disgusted. "Let them have it and welcome to it."

"And your brother?"

"Same thing. He's my brother, but let's face it—he's got to try harder, like Avis."

"You're saying he needs a gimmick, too."

"Rebecca, my brother's my brother, but we haven't really been close for a long time. He's made it clear nothing would make him happier than running me out of business. If he thinks that starter can do it . . ." He stopped for a moment and finished in a much lower voice, "I pity him."

"He makes a nice loaf."

"It's not good enough to hurt me." He snapped out the words. "Tony and Thompson can battle it out for all I care. I'm not going to get involved in some kind of petty puff-up that's getting people killed."

"So you think Peter was killed because of the starter," I said.

"It sounds," said Chris, "as if you think your own brother might have done it."

"My own . . . Now you listen to me, young lady—"

"Don't you young-lady me, you big galumph."

"Galoot," I blurted, and started laughing. Chris really had a terrible time with words.

But I was the only one laughing. Bob was suddenly very serious. "I'm sorry, Chris. It just slipped out. But you did accuse me of accusing my own brother of murder."

"Not quite. I was just trying to clarify things."

"Okay, let me make it clear that I wasn't accusing Tony of anything."

"I'm sorry." Chris spoke in a small voice. She hated apologizing.

I said, "Aren't you forgetting something? There was a fourth bidder, you know." I don't know why I said that. I had no wish to accuse Sally Devereaux of murder. It just made me mad, the macho way he seemed to imagine the men duking it out among themselves.

Bob leaned back in his Naugahyde chair and swiveled sideways so he wasn't facing us. "Sally Devereaux," he said, almost wonderingly. "Yes, I did forget." He swiveled back. "I guess I don't think of her as much competition, as far as business goes. But come to think of it, maybe Peter *was* involved in a triangle. Or something."

I spoke quickly, sensing Chris's distress. "What do you mean?"

"You didn't know they'd been lovers?"

"Peter and Sally?" But even as I said it, I remembered Peter's discomfort when she'd barged in on us the night before the auction, how eager he was to get rid of her.

Bob nodded. "Peter dumped her."

CHAPTER 8

"He's awful," said Chris, back in the Volvo.

"Chris, are you sure you want to go on with this?"

"I don't care about Sally and Peter. Not much, anyway—at least their affair argues he wasn't gay."

It didn't, I thought, but I let it go.

"I just hate guys like that Bob Tosi, that's all. So damned sure of himself. Calling me 'young lady'!"

I put the car in reverse and backed out of the parking space. "I don't think he's so bad. He probably grew up in a very sexist milieu. To hear Anita tell it, that's how Italian families are."

"If I needed that kind of ratatool, I could have stayed in Virginia."

"That kind of what?"

"Crap!"

"It's not like anyone's asking you to go out with him."

"Go out with him! I wouldn't go out with him if he picked me up and threw me over his shoulder."

"Okay, okay. What do you want to do instead?"

"Let's go see Tony. Maybe he's nicer."

"It's almost five o'clock—traffic on the bridge'll be awful. Let's try Clayton Thompson."

We drove to the Stanford Court, and I asked for Thompson on the house phone. He'd checked out.

"Has he gone back to New York?" As soon as it was out of my mouth, I realized the operator couldn't possibly know. But she surprised me: "No, ma'am. He left a forwarding address in the Eureka Valley—at the home of Mr. and Mrs. Richard Richards.''

The Eureka Valley is in the city's Castro district, the city's gay ghetto, but a few young married types who'd bought property there before the gays took over in full force still lived there. Some women said they loved it because the streets were always crowded—and not with rapists.

Mr. and Mrs. Richards didn't seem to be among the property owners. The address we had was an apartment building, about half a block from Castro Street itself, the center of all the action. There probably wasn't a rapist within eight or ten blocks. Mrs. Richards must love it, but I wondered if it didn't make her husband a bit uneasy.

As we got out of the Volvo, we saw Clayton Thompson walking toward us with a load of groceries. A man in a leather jacket was walking toward him.

''Clayton!'' called Chris, just as the other man caught up with him. He turned, saw us, started to smile, then turned back, apparently listening to something the man was saying.

Suddenly he shoved the groceries at the other man, hollered, ''Run, y'all. He's got a gun!'' and started toward us at a gallop.

I saw the other man go down, and then I followed orders. I turned and ran toward the safety of crowded Castro, high heels clicking, Chris at my side, and Clayton catching up fast.

I heard the other man swear, grunt as he stood up, and then I heard his footsteps behind us. I ran faster, thinking I'd probably manifested the mugger in some mystical way, being so relaxed about rapists. It served me right for getting too sure of myself.

We rounded the corner onto Castro, and still we heard pursuing footsteps. There seemed nothing to do but go into a bar. Clearly the streets weren't safe. I charged into the nearest one, Chris and Clayton right behind me. Practically everyone in there was wearing jeans and trendy haircut; everyone—and I mean, bar none—was male and looked under thirty. So you could say we caused quite a stir—two women and a middle-aged man in a business suit. Only it didn't take the usual form of a stir. It took the form of cold, dead, unwelcoming silence.

The place was mobbed, too. It was just the cocktail hour, and guys were practically sitting in each other's laps. There was hardly room for the indigenous ferns. We started elbowing our way through the crowd—anything to get out of the doorway. I think I had in mind we could use the phone to call police, but basically, I was on automatic pilot. I was just moving. I kept looking over my shoulder, imagining our pursuer might follow us in there—silly thought, really. What mugger would do that? Then I saw him, just coming in the door.

I nudged Clayton. "Omigod," he shouted. "He's got a gun!"

Since everyone was giving us the silent treatment, you can imagine how that went over. Yelling "Fire!" in a crowded theater was good social manners by comparison. Tables turned over as some guys tried to dive under them, and others got up to jump the gunman. In about half a second the scene was like a barroom brawl in a movie.

Some guys, in their rush to get to the baddy, bashed into other guys, who responded by slugging them. Their buddies responded by slugging back. Forty or fifty different private fights seemed to have broken out at once. Someone went through the front window in an earsplitting smash of glass.

Chris hit the floor as a chair fell against her. A guy with his fist raised stood over her. I slammed him one on the arm. "You want to hit a woman, hit me, you momser!"

Clayton, ever the southern gent, pulled me back, looked straight into the guy's eyes, and said, "You'll have to excuse my friend. She's a little upset."

I was sure that was an invitation to get killed, but the guy just muttered, "Sheeit!" and turned away, arms flailing, looking for a target worthy of him.

The bartender, wearing a white apron, came up behind Chris and started to help her up. "Everyone's a little on edge," he said.

I almost laughed. On edge, indeed. Teeth were being lost left and right.

"Come on." The bartender herded the three of us like a brooding hen. He was far and away the burliest guy in the place. His idea was to take us out the back way, but it was blocked.

There were only two guys standing in front of the entrance to the space behind the bar, though. They both had their fists up and they were circling like boxers. The bartender banged their heads together and stepped over their supine forms. "Back here."

We stepped behind the bar, stooping down for safety. The bartender went for a telephone, but sirens sounded in the distance and he abandoned the effort. Someone sailed over the bar, lay there a second, then sat up and shook his head, probably trying to clear it. You'd think the sound of the sirens might have sobered people up, but nothing doing. They kept mixing it up, maybe even going at it a little harder, as if they knew their fighting time was limited.

The bartender, apparently trying to do what he could to restore peace, again cleared the pathway between the bar and the rest of the room, and we saw that there was a tiny space to the back entrance. This time Clayton said, "Come on," and took the lead. He pushed bodies out of his way, and we were out.

Out of the barroom, anyway. We were in a dark passage, and, believe it or not, it was blocked by two young men necking like teenagers, kissing and feeling each other up.

" 'Scuse us," said Clayton, but they didn't budge.

"Let us through, please," Chris said. One man put his hand in the back of the other one's jeans. I know some people are turned on by violence, but this was ridiculous. However, if it was violence they wanted, it was violence they were going to get: I kicked first one in the shin, then the other.

"What the hell?" said the first one, and turned toward us, fists clenched. But his friend, apparently miffed at the interruption, pulled him out of the way. "Let them through."

And then we were really outside.

We leaned up against the side of the building, catching our breath for a moment. "Let's get out of here," said Clayton. "There's gon' be a stampede out that back door when those cops get here."

We were barely ahead of the stampede. Cops chased the stampeders, but we simply stood aside and let them pass, figuring we'd probably be taken for tourists who'd lost their way. It seemed to work.

When we were alone, Clayton asked, "Y'all want a drink? Anywhere but this neighborhood. What kind of place is this? There goes a guy with two shades of eyeshadow."

Chris and I couldn't help laughing—it was the universal out-of-towner's response to Castro Street. We may have been a little rude, but a laugh at his expense was a small thing, and it made me feel better. I was upset with Clayton—he might not have meant to, but he'd started a near-riot.

We found a quiet bar in the adjoining Noe Valley, and when Chris had her bourbon and Clayton and I our white wines, I asked Clayton exactly what was going on.

He shrugged. "I guess I kind of lost control. Guy tried to mug me—you saw it."

"What did he say to you?"

"Asked for my money, that's all. Had his hand in his jacket like he had a gun. Scared hell out of me. I've been feeling a little funny in that neighborhood anyway. Can't think why Rick and Mary live there—with a baby, too."

Chris nodded, wise with an insider's knowledge. "That's probably why. It's hard for people with children to find apartments in San Francisco."

"Must be. That's all I can say."

"Listen, Clayton," I said. "We were coming to see you because we've got something to tell you." I told him about the second starter.

"Well, glory be. My comp'ny's gon' be mighty happy to hear about that." He sighed. "I was gon' take a few days off, stayin' with my friends. But I guess it'll have to wait awhile. What's the legal procedure on that starter?"

"The court will appoint an administrator for the estate," said Chris. "That is, if it turns out Peter did die intestate—and I suppose his apartment's been searched by now. If there's no will there—or anywhere—that's the procedure."

"Any chance one of y'all'll be appointed? You, Chris? You were Martinelli's lawyer."

She shook her head. "No. It has to be Peter's sister, Anita Ashton. She's his nearest relative, so she stands to inherit."

"Unfortunately," I said, "I'm afraid in a case like this—when a woman is appointed—it's called an 'administratrix.' "

"A bit archaic." Thompson sounded distracted. "So if my comp'ny still wants a chance at that starter, I s'pose the person to approach is this Ms. Ashton."

We nodded. "But I happened to talk with her today, and I don't think she'll want to sell. A private sale isn't possible at this point, anyway—not till the estate is probated."

"Never too soon to start thinkin' about it, is it? I think my comp'ny'll make her a mighty handsome offer."

CHAPTER 9

We excused ourselves, stopped at a gas station, and looked up Tony Tosi in the phone book. He lived in the Sunset, the relentlessly middle-class district south of Golden Gate Park. The houses there give the famous ticky-tacky ones of Daly City a run for their money, though they do have bay windows. Many of them have no front yards, and they butt up against each other like town houses. The area looks so barren visitors sometimes think they've hit the sixth borough of New York, but if you stand in the kitchen of a Sunset house and look out the window, you can see green for blocks—everyone has a long skinny backyard.

There's not much traffic in the Sunset, not much crime, and hardly any sunsets that anyone can see. San Francisco weather varies from neighborhood to neighborhood, and some of the worst plagues the Sunset, which is sometimes known as Fogville.

The young woman who opened the Tosi door was short and blond. And bland. At least that was my unkind take on her—anybody that cute and bouncy must be bland. I really ought to reform sometime, but meeting Cathy Tosi didn't provide much inspiration for it. On closer inspection, it turned out she was bland.

When she smiled, she showed a mouthful of perfect teeth. She had on a sort of honey-beige lambswool sweater that said, "Look at me—I'm fluffy and cute," in case the casual observer were half-blind or something. She was remarkably similar to Sally Devereaux, but nearly ten years younger.

Cathy took our names, seemed to recognize Chris's, and went in search of Tony, leaving us in a sort of gold brocade wonderland. The living-room curtains were gold brocade and so was the sofa and so were the chairs. The carpet was gold wool, probably of very good quality, as were the various mass-produced dark wood tables in the room. There was a bit of Steuben glass, some heavy glass vases with bubbles in them, and on one wall was a reproduction of van Gogh's *Sunflowers*. I couldn't tell if it had been selected to go with the gold furnishings or the other way around.

Tony came in, apparently from some TV-equipped room at the rear of the house. He wore a Ralph Lauren polo shirt, and a pair of Calvin Klein jeans, and he had a gold chain around his neck and a Rolex watch on his wrist. I was sure that if there were any way to get a plain gold chain with a manufacturer's label on it, Tony would have done it.

I had the same feeling I'd had before—that Tony was less substantial than Bob. But I could see the outline of his body very well underneath the polo shirt, and he certainly worked out, whether Bob did or not. Maybe Bob was a trifle over-weight. Or maybe it wasn't physical at all. Maybe it was the fact that Bob always seemed at ease, Tony perennially worried.

"Hi, Chris," he said. "Rebecca. Is anything wrong?"

"Not at all," said Chris. "We have some good news for you."

"Can I get you anything?" asked Cathy.

It was the cocktail hour, but both Chris and I asked for coffee, hoping that would take longer, giving us an excuse to stay and make apparent small talk after we'd stated our business.

We were already on the sofa, and Tony sat down in one of the gold-brocade chairs. He looked out of place there, but I suppose Chris and I did, too. It wasn't a room you could get comfortable in.

"The starter's been found," said Chris.

Tony's face said it wished we would speak English. He was quiet for a while, apparently doing a slow translation, and when he finally spoke, it wasn't worth waiting for. He said, "Oh?"

"The cryogenics firm had another batch," Chris continued.

Cathy reappeared with the coffee. "Cream? Sugar?" That occupied the next few minutes, and I got the idea Tony was glad for some time to think. When he spoke again, he looked like a little kid begging for a new bike but pretty sure Mom and Dad couldn't afford it. "I know you don't know me," he said, "and I don't know how to say this, but . . . look, I want to tell you some things."

Chris and I nodded, wearing our most sympathetic-lawyer looks. "I want to tell you about my brother and me." His hand shook as he put his coffee cup on the table. "Bobby's the oldest, you know what I mean? I always looked up to him, kind of let him tell me what to do and how to do it when we were kids. I sort of got in the habit of it. So everybody in the family, they always thought Bobby was smarter and kind of more . . . competent." He made a face as he said the last word, as if it had given him trouble sometime.

"I guess I thought so, too," he continued. "I mean, I guess it was me that gave them that idea in the first place, know what I mean?" Again, we nodded. "So, anyway, Bobby was kind of the favorite and he kind of knew it, I guess. But we both went into the business—I don't mean the baking business; I mean the family business, the Tosi Bakery." His shoulders straightened a bit when he said, "Tosi Bakery," as if it were his instead of his brother's.

"We got to be damn good bakers, you know that? I mean, Bobby and me both. I'm gonna tell you something—Bobby can't bake any better than I can." He sighed. "It's like when we were kids. People think he can, because he's got the *Tosi* Bakery, you know what I mean? But he's no better. In fact, I'm putting out a superior product right this minute." He nodded, emphasizing the point. "You can run a taste test. Go ahead. Try Bobby's loaf and mine, and see which is better. Guarantee you Palermo makes a better sourdough. Go ahead. Try it yourself."

"We will," I said, because it didn't look as if he were going to continue until he had our word on a taste test. I presumed we couldn't have one there and then, because there was no Tosi bread in the household.

"Know why it's better? Because of the secret ingredient, that's why. Look, it's this way. My brother and me came up together. We learned to bake from the same teacher—our papa, who was the best baker in town except for old man Martinelli. So it stands to reason we'd bake the same, doesn't it?" He looked at us anxiously.

Once again, we nodded.

"Unless," he said, straightening up again and looking triumphant, "unless what?"

"I can't imagine," said Chris.

"Unless one of us improved on the old way. Know what I mean?"

There was nothing to do except nod again. My head was starting to feel like a yoyo.

"Well, I improved on it. Go ahead. Try a taste test, you'll see."

"You mean," I said, "that you've added something to the bread that you don't ordinarily find in sourdough?"

"I didn't say that," said Tony, looking mischievous and quite pleased with himself. I glanced at Cathy and saw that she looked anxious.

"But you mentioned a secret ingredient."

"Ah. You noticed that, did you?"

Guess what I did then? Right you are—I nodded.

"The secret ingredient's what does it. Nobody knows what it is and nobody's gonna know—except Cathy, of course." He patted Cathy's knee. "But it's the thing that makes the Palermo loaf the best. The only thing is, we aren't the biggest."

"Why," asked Chris, "did you leave the Tosi Bakery?"

"I was getting to that. Like I was saying, me and my brother went into the business. And then Pop died. Mama, she didn't know nothin' about running the business, so her and Pop had things figured out what would happen in the event of his death. It was in his will and everything—me and Bobby inherited everything, split right down the middle. Equal shares of the Tosi Bakery. Equal partners. But somebody had to be president of the corporation, and that was Bobby. So there we were grown up and Bobby was still my boss. And I had all these great ideas about how to run a bakery. I wanted to expand, build a couple of new plants, truck bread all over the state, you know? Bobby wouldn't buy it.''

For once, Chris and I got to shake our heads.

''Bobby was so used to me being little brother and everything, he wouldn't listen to me at all. So we fought all the time. And Mama, she was no help. She'd just say, 'Now, Tony, you listen to your brother. Bobby's always been the smart one.' So pretty soon I couldn't take it anymore, you know what I mean? I mean, I could bake as good as Bobby and I could run a business just as good. Only everybody thought I was 'little brother' and I couldn't think for myself.''

''So you had to get out,'' I said.

Now it was Tony's turn to nod, and he did it emphatically. ''Yeah. I had to go.''

''Bobby bought you out?''

''It wasn't quite that simple. See, I didn't want to go. I mean, I guess you ladies can't understand, not being Italian or anything, but this was our family business—the *Tosi* Bakery. I couldn't leave it, just like that—that was the last thing I wanted to do.'' He sighed again. ''I'm a self-made man now, you know? Even Bobby can't say that. I'm a real high achiever. But you know what? I'd give it all up just to have the family business back.''

''I don't understand,'' said Chris. ''You said you had to get out.''

''I mean I was forced out.'' He held up a hand. ''I'm not accusing Bobby of anything—it was all fair and square—it's just not the choice I'd have made, that's all.''

''What happened?''

''Well, I asked Bobby to buy me out. Of course he wouldn't, but he really did want me to leave. I mean, somebody had to go, that was obvious, and neither of us wanted to start a new bakery. Both of us wanted that one."

"Yes?"

"Of course, now that I think of it, I'm pretty sure I wanted that Tosi Bakery a hell of a lot more than Bobby ever did. He was already the family's fair-haired boy and everything—he didn't have anything to prove; I was the one who did. If he'd been the one to leave, he'd probably have done it a lot more easily than I did—I mean, he considered it a kind of pleasant challenge rather than"—he seemed at a loss for words—"than what you have to do to survive." He paused and his voice dropped. "It's survival to me, and it still scares the hell out of me."

Looking at him, I could believe it. He was fidgeting with his coffee cup, and the swarthy Tosi hide looked almost pale. It was apparently very hard for him to talk about—probably even think about—these things. I figured he must be doing it for a reason and he'd get to that pretty soon. But there was still something about this part of it that I didn't get.

"How," I asked, "did your brother get you to leave?"

"Well, he didn't exactly *get* me to leave. Like I said, I think he was sort of willing to be the one that left. But he won the toss."

"I beg your pardon?"

"Finally, it just got ridiculous and there didn't seem anything else to do without a lot of dumb lawsuits. So we flipped a coin."

I let out a whoosh of breath, but Chris was on top of the thing fast. "Let me guess," she said. "It was Robert's idea, right?"

"How'd you know?"

"Oh, just a thought. So winning the toss gave him the right to buy you out, is that it?"

"Right. He even offered to lend me money to start a new bakery, but I wouldn't take it. I didn't want to owe him anymore. In fact—I guess you know this—we don't talk much anymore."

"We heard that."

"It's no big fight, really. He's asked me to lunch a few times, and every now and then I've gone. It's just that I find him so damned . . ."

"Arrogant?" asked Chris.

"Exactly! You're reading my mind."

She smiled modestly. "Just a good guesser."

"Well, anyway, what I was getting to—I've been pretty scared, starting Palermo and all." His wife reached out and took his hand. He paused, as if he'd lost his place. Then he said, "You know? Real scared. It's the toughest thing I've ever done. And I'm doing good. I'm doing real good. I've got this house and a beautiful wife and all the nice clothes I could want and a Mercedes. And I've got the second most successful bakery in San Francisco and the best bread." He was sweating, speaking slowly. "But I'm still scared. I'm afraid I'm gonna lose it all. I'm afraid one day I'll wake up and it won't be there. Somehow, it just doesn't seem like it was written for the younger Tosi kid—the dumb one—to make it like this. You know? It's like I can't quite believe it; like I'm afraid I'll wake up someday and find it all gone." He stopped and looked at us with pleading eyes. "You know?"

We nodded on cue.

"So, listen, I really need that starter. It might give me just the little edge I need—I mean, if I had it, I *know*, I just *know* that would take care of things."

"Take care of things?"

"Then people would believe, see? I mean, I already have the best sourdough, but nobody realizes that because they think 'Tosi Bakery, Tosi's tops.' But if I had that starter, they'd *have* to believe, you see what I mean?" He kept talking, fast, not even giving us time to nod. "So, listen, could you possibly give me a break? Just a little break? I'm willing to pay top dollar—no one'll get cheated, that's the last thing I want. But please sell me that starter. Please?"

I felt embarrassed, as if we'd misrepresented ourselves. "Tony, I'm awfully sorry," I said, "but Anita Ashton will almost certainly inherit it—you'll have to deal with her. We didn't mean to give you the impression we actually had any power in this. All we wanted to do was let you know there was a second batch of starter."

He looked crestfallen. "Oh. I guess I should have realized that. I got kind of carried away."

"We certainly have all the sympathy in the world for your position. But we also should tell you that we've just come from telling Clayton Thompson. He sounded as if he intends to make Anita an offer."

"Thompson? Oh yeah—the Conglomerate Foods guy."

"And I'm afraid," said Chris, "it's our job to tell the others as well."

He sighed, and when he spoke, he sounded bitter. "Ah, yes," he said. "The rest of the family."

"And Sally Devereaux, of course."

"She's family."

"I beg your pardon?"

Tony looked surprised. "Didn't you know? She's Bobby's ex—the former Mrs. Robert Tosi. Listen, I really do bake better bread than Bobby. Why don't you ladies come to the plant for a tour—tomorrow, say? Or next week maybe. Whenever you like—I want to show you what I can do."

We said we'd try to make it.

CHAPTER 10

Nothing now was going to keep us from Sally. I let Chris out to get us a snack to keep our strength up. She came back with two loaves of bread, a Tosi and a Palermo. "For the taste test," she said.

"But Wednesday's no day to buy French bread."

"What do you mean?"

"Didn't you know? The bread truck drivers take Wednesdays and Sundays off. So the bakeries close down on Tuesdays and Saturdays. Ergo, any bread you buy on Wednesday or Sunday is a day old."

"Let's try it anyway. It's an hour's drive to Sonoma." She handed me a hunk. Day old or not, it held up nicely. Good dark crust, nice tangy interior. I asked for a second piece and wolfed that one down, too.

"Good," I said. "Whose bread was it?"

"Both."

"You mean I had bread from both loaves? I'd have sworn both pieces came from the same bakery."

"So much for Tony's secret ingredient."

Sally lived a few miles outside Sonoma, in the Valley of the Moon near Glen Ellen. In the daytime we could have seen the vineyards that take up every inch of available space in the wine country, but it was nearly nine and long since dark by the time we arrived.

The house was modern, ordinary, with aluminum window frames and no shutters. Apparently, Sally didn't live there alone—there was a bicycle out front. A small voice answered our ring: "Who's there?"

"We're here to see your mom."

The door opened, displaying one of the prettiest children I'd ever seen—a boy about eight years old—but then, I'm a sucker for dark hair and blue eyes. Sally came up behind him. "Hi, I wasn't expecting you."

"We have some good news for you."

"I could use some. I just turned on the radio and heard about the starter disappearing. Would you like some pâté?"

Within seconds, Sally had laid a small feast on her long smooth pine table—pâté, butter, cornichons, a little white wine, and her own sourdough. I tried the bread with a little butter first, not polluting it with pâté. It was like candy.

I can't explain it exactly—it wasn't sweet or anything, but so melt-in-your-mouth perfect that that's what came to mind. I said, "Chris. Try this bread. You won't believe it."

As Chris did, Sally leaned forward, hands twitching. She watched Chris taste and hardly gave her time to swallow before she spoke: "Do you think it's okay?"

"It's the greatest," said Chris. "Nobody else is making anything like it."

I helped myself to more, this time with pâté. "Is it because the other bakeries are so big? You have better quality control?"

Sally shook her head. "I could bake just as good a bread if I had to do it in million-loaf batches. If only I had the opportunity."

"Why on earth," asked Chris, "do you want the Martinelli starter? You honestly think you could improve on this?"

"You really think it's that good?"

"You know it is."

Tears stood in her eyes. "The way things work in this country, a thing is good if people think so. You've got to have a gimmick. A scam, to get their attention."

"You feel you haven't had the recognition you deserve," I said. "Is that it?"

"I can barely afford to pay my gas bills—Bob and Tony

are millionaires. Or Bob is anyway, and Tony's got a Mercedes.''

"And you think if you had the starter other people would think your bread was special?''

She nodded.

"What we came for," I said, "is to tell you there was a second batch of starter. Whoever stole it didn't get it all.''

She looked like a woman who'd just been told her child wasn't on that wrecked schoolbus after all. While I explained the situation, tears ran down her face. "There's a chance," she said. "Oh, God, there's still a chance.''

"You want that starter in the worst way," I said. I've often noticed that if you just say what you're thinking about people, they somehow get the idea they owe you an explanation.

The kid came in for a bite of pâté and saw his mom crying. "Mommy, what's wrong?''

She wiped her eyes. "Nothing, Bobby—go watch TV, okay?" She turned back to us. "Or nothing new, anyway. You're right, Rebecca—I really do want that starter in the worst way. I want to be the biggest, best, most important sourdough baker in the history of the world. I want to go down in history that way.''

"You're probably already the best.''

"Not good enough. No one knows about me. Do you know where I learned to bake?''

"You were married to Robert Tosi, weren't you?''

"That's right. He taught me the business. I think he thought it was cute, or I was doing it to be supportive or it was a hobby or something." She broke off another piece of bread for herself. "I guess it was at first. I was an ace cook—I mean I still am. I made the pâté as well as the bread, by the way. I was a good little wife who always did the wifely thing, and cooking was wifely. But I was really *good* at it. So I thought it might be fun to learn to bake sourdough. Bob gave me a job—actually paid me to work at the bakery till I'd learned what I wanted to. When we split up, I had to be a baker. It was the only trade I had.''

Chris asked, "Did you plan it that way?''

"In a way I did. I wasn't very happy married to Bob—I mean, after Bobby was about three. I needed something else. I have a degree in sociology, but—I don't know—being a social worker didn't appeal to me. I needed something I could do on my own—and I was already a great cook. Bob was a baker, and it was just sort of *there*."

She looked down at the floor. "I don't suppose I was consciously thinking about leaving him then, but I guess it was in the back of my mind."

"You were the one who left?"

Sally nodded. Her eyes filled up again. "It was awful. He wanted me to do nothing but stick around the house. He had no sense of my needs at all."

Chris patted her hand. She had all the sympathy in the world for anyone who'd suffered at the hands of the Dread Tosi Monster. "You're nice," said Sally suddenly. "Were you seeing Peter?"

"Yes. I was very fond of him."

"I guess he told you about me?"

Chris shook her head. "Peter wasn't like that."

"How could I forget? Of course he wasn't. He wouldn't tell you his name if he thought he could avoid it. We hardly ever saw each other, the last year or so, but he was a wonderful person. Who'd want to kill someone like that?"

She sipped some wine and went into a little reverie. "Peter was the reason I left Bob. I mean, I needed to leave. I wasn't happy with Bob. But I just didn't have the courage. Peter courted me. He took me on picnics and things, at first just acting like a good friend, and then we became lovers. He simply took me away from Bob. He wouldn't be stopped."

Chris looked as if she were about to lose consciousness.

"I guess I used him, in a way, to give myself the courage to leave—I leaned on him. But he fell too much in love with me."

Obviously Chris couldn't speak, so I did: "You didn't love him?"

"Oh, I guess I did, in a way. But not—you know—the way I'd really like to love somebody. I just couldn't open up to

him. And I always thought it was silly the way he fought with
Anita. I like Anita a lot, and I didn't think it was right, a
brother and sister being estranged like that. I tried to get him
to make up with her, but he wouldn't.''

"That was why you couldn't fall in love with him?"

"It sounds odd, doesn't it? But I think it had something to
do with it. He just wasn't emotionally mature.''

Chris sighed and nodded. Apparently, she identified with
Sally.

"So I had to let him down gently,'' Sally continued.

"But surely that wasn't all,'' I said. "Did Peter seem
slightly cold to you? I don't know how to ask this gently, but
did you get the feeling he might have been bisexual?"

"Peter?'' Sally laughed. "Never. He was crazy about me
and showed it in every way. I mean, *every* way. He took it
kind of hard when I stopped seeing him. I don't think he had
another girl friend until you, Chris. I think you must be a
very special person.'' She gave Chris a very warm smile.
"It wasn't easy to get Peter's attention.''

Chris started puddling up, so I changed the subject. "If
Anita decided to sell the starter, you'd want to bid, is that
right?''

"I don't think she'd want to sell it. But maybe, just
maybe—''

"Well, going back to the original auction—the others must
have stacks of money at their disposal. I don't mean to be
rude, but could you really have hoped to outbid them?"

"I'd have tried, anyhow.''

"You're awfully brave,'' I said, and meant it.

"Thanks.'' Sally smiled. "It's hard to keep my nerve up.
I don't think I could have done it without support.''

"Support? You mean from your friends?''

She looked flustered. "I have someone who believes in
me.''

"Ah. A backer.''

Her cheeks were slightly pink and she smiled like a teenager. "You might call it that. But if I didn't believe in my
product so much, I couldn't possibly have accepted help. It's

so hard for me—it's something I have to learn. Anyway, this is a good friend, but our arrangement was also a good business deal for both of us—I believe that or I wouldn't have been in it."

Bobby came into the kitchen, dragging an old worn blanket and rubbing his eyes. "Hi, young man," said Sally. "Time for you to go to bed."

Chris and I stood up, recognizing our exit cue. "Did you really like my bread?" asked Sally.

"It's wonderful," said Chris.

"Well, you must take some with you." Sally went to a cabinet and produced two loaves. "One for each of you. Fresh-baked."

Headed south in the Volvo, Chris said, "I like her."

"She's disarming, isn't she? Tony was honest, but he seemed on the ragged edge. Sally just seemed kind of confused and not very bright. Things seem to pour out of her because that's the way she is."

"I felt very sorry for her when she talked about Peter."

"If I were you, I don't think that would have been my reaction."

"She's kidding herself, Rebecca. I think she's remembering Peter as a great deal more ardent than he could possibly have been—remember, I knew him pretty well. Sort of."

"Maybe she was lying. Bob Tosi said Peter dumped her— maybe she's telling it the other way around because she doesn't want us to know she's got a murder motive."

"Listen—knowing Peter, he'd never have told anybody who dumped whom—it just wasn't his style. And Bob would assume Peter dumped Sally because he's macho and macho men always dump their women."

"But Sally dumped *him*."

"Well, he'd like to think men dump women. It's pretty odd, don't you think, that of the four potential bidders he's the only one who's really accepted the fact there's probably not going to be a new auction? I think he's got what he wants. The auction's stopped and the Tosi Bakery remains on top.

When you think of it, he has the best motive of the four of them. He doesn't need the starter to stay on top—he just needs to see that no one else gets it.''

"You think he stole it?"

"One of them did."

As we were crossing the bridge, Chris said, "I can't get Sally out of my mind. She's so sad."

"How do you mean?"

"She wants to be an independent woman so badly—and she has a lot of talent; no question she makes the best bread of them all. But she seems so dependent on men."

"That's been bothering me, too. Her husband was a baker, so she became one. Then she couldn't leave him till she had another man. And now she's got a backer. You know what's the saddest part of it? Did you notice the way she kept asking us whether or not we really liked her sourdough? Deep down, she doesn't really believe in that bread."

I dropped Chris off, found my parking place taken, and finally managed to get another one (no mean feat in North Beach). Then I stumbled up my stairs, exhausted, and turned on my message machine. What I heard didn't make me happy.

Rob had called. He was furious that I hadn't told him about the second starter. The worst of it was, he was right. And he didn't even know I'd failed to tip him on another hot story. I dialed the familiar number. "I forgot you, pussycat. I'm sorry."

"Don't 'pussycat' me, you traitor. This is a huge story, don't you understand? And it's my story. And you're my girl friend, and you forgot me."

"I've been kind of busy. Did you hear about the brawl on Castro Street?"

"Hear about it? I covered it. Some idiot yelled something about a gun and all hell broke loose."

"Did anyone have a gun?"

"No. But the guy who was supposed to has a broken jaw. And half the pretty boys in the Castro got their noses smashed."

"I was there."

"You were *what*? Rebecca, where's your loyalty? Why didn't you call me, dammit?"

"Listen, you don't need me. You got both your stories, right? The second starter and the brawl. How'd you do that?"

"Sources. I'm a reporter, remember? I'm supposed to know how to get information."

"My point exactly. Now, shall I tell you about my day?"

Naturally, he was all ears. The part that intrigued him the most was Clayton's claiming the man in the leather jacket was trying to mug him. The man told police he'd simply asked for the time, and had chased us into the bar because Clayton threw a bag of groceries at him for no reason.

"Well, he would say that, wouldn't he? Wouldn't you if you were a mugger?"

"I guess so. Want to come to dinner tomorrow?"

I said I did. I had to argue a divorce case the next day and I could use a home-cooked meal.

CHAPTER 11

Rob lives on Cathedral Hill in a weird building with a great view. What makes the building weird is that it's round. Otherwise, it's just a characterless modern building. But it does have that view, and as for its banality, Rob says a person with an overactive imagination—such as himself—is stimulated by the ordinary. I'm not too sure what he means by that, but I'll tell you one thing—if we ever decide to formalize our acquaintanceship, it's not going to be there. I can tolerate it just about long enough for dinner.

We had chicken that night. I happen to remember that because it's all Rob ever makes. I know he knows how to make at least four or five things, because every once in a while he has. But usually he just pops a chicken in the oven with some potatoes and onions. This he serves on an oak table that also doubles as his desk and fits into a corner of his very masculine living room.

Why do single men always have fake leather sofas? Do they think the Bachelors' Union will drum them out if they sit on velveteen or corduroy? Rob's got one just like all the others, and also a lot of books and a terrific painting of kachinas by a Hopi artist. When you turn off the lights and light a couple of candles, it's quite a cozy place for dinner. If you also open the curtains, it's one of the wonders of the world.

We had a nice Chardonnay with our dinner, and after coffee I felt a lot like curling up on the fake leather sofa, maybe watching the lights for an hour or two. I am not what you call a night person.

Rob, on the other hand, probably wouldn't go to bed at all if he could find anyone who'd stay up and keep him company. He gets his second wind after dinner and then wants to dance the night away. I planned to put my foot down tonight. It was going to be a quiet evening or he was going to spend the rest of it alone.

He reached over and tweaked my chin. "Wake up there."

I closed my eyes and let my shoulders sag. "Uh-uh. Not on your life."

"Uh-huh. Absolutely. We've got places to go and things to see."

"Rob, honey, I just don't feel like—"

"Yes, you do. This you'll like, I promise you. We're going to a secret hiding place."

My eyes came open. He was already up and putting on his coat. "Beg your pardon? Did you say secret hiding place?"

"I did. We're going to have an adventure." He held out my new charcoal-gray suede jacket, which I'd gotten half price for $150 and which I loved so much I put it on automatically.

"I thought only kids had secret hiding places."

He turned out the lights and held the door open. "Kids and some grown-ups."

We were in the elevator before I thought to ask, "Why do we need to hide?"

"We don't. At least I don't think so."

"Then why are we going there?"

"I told you. To have an adventure. It's somewhere neither of us has ever been before."

"Don't be too sure. I'm a Bay Area native."

"Here's a hint: It's near China Basin."

In that case, he was almost certainly right about my not having been there—it's not the sort of place a lady lawyer goes unless she's lunching at Blanche's, an eccentric but much-favored restaurant in the warehouse district. Which is what the area around the China Basin is. All of a sudden I had it: "It's where the second starter is."

He tapped his nose. "On the schnoz."

"How'd you find out?"

He shrugged. "Sources."

"Come on. What sources?"

"Well, actually, I just kept asking around until I found someone who had a friend who works at Fail-Safe. One of the copy boys."

"And?"

"And it turns out it's no big-deal secret at all—they have two warehouses, and some things are stored in one, some in another. If the control starter wasn't in the main building—which it wouldn't have been, because then it wouldn't have been a control—it had to be in the other. The company's just being tight-lipped because they figure they've got a security problem."

I thought about that for a moment. "Something tells me," I said, "that I didn't get a full and complete answer to one of my previous questions. So I repeat: Why are we going there?"

"Well, I'm doing a little story about cryogenics—sort of a sidebar to run with the ongoing sourdough saga—and I thought I'd like to see what the place looks like."

"Why don't you just ask for a tour?"

"I did. No dice."

"So you're going to describe it from the outside—'in a rundown warehouse near China Basin' sort of thing?"

"If that's all we get, sure. I thought we might check out the security, maybe—who knows? At least we can see what's around it and I can describe that."

"Are you going to publish the address?"

He didn't answer for a while. When he spoke, it was in kind of a clipped way, designed to discourage further probing: "I haven't decided yet."

I wasn't sufficiently discouraged. "What purpose would it serve?"

He sighed with the air of a person who has explained a

thing to a child a hundred times. "Credibility, Rebecca. If I give the address, I really saw *it*, not just any rundown warehouse in China Basin."

"But maybe the thief will see it and get the control. Or maybe he'll try and some innocent guard will interfere and get killed."

"That's not a journalistic problem." He spoke in the same clipped tone, and I wanted to shake him. Reporters never seem to care what kind of chaos is unleashed as a result of their handiwork; every day they open a new and different Pandora's Box and don't give a damn about the consequences. It was the main problem I had with Rob; if he weren't a reporter, he'd be perfect.

I kept my mouth shut until we pulled up in front of a properly rundown warehouse. It's a hideous neighborhood, that one, a place of things, not people. There's a spooky old railroad switchyard there, and the San Francisco RV Park, where the old Southern Pacific Station used to be. Also, there are two bridges across China Basin itself, which is a little finger of the bay. The Peter R. Maloney Bridge, hard by Blanche's, is really part of Fourth Street, and my personal favorite, the Francis "Lefty" O'Doul Bridge, is part of Third.

Mostly, there are a lot of warehouses of varying sizes and conditions of decay. The place always seems dead to me, even in the daytime, when occasional human beings and dozens of cars dot the landscape. At night, it can oppress you like a paper bag over your head. What little light there is gets swallowed up by a large and mighty blackness.

So we couldn't see much after Rob turned off his headlights. "Is this it?" I said.

Rob shook his head.

At first I thought he was making fun of me for asking such a dumb question, but no—he pointed down the block to our left. "I don't want to alert the guard if there is one. Let's walk over quietly."

We both had on jogging shoes, so quiet was easy. We were

just a couple of cats slinking on little fog feet, and suddenly I was having fun again.

I forgot I was mad at Rob. I forgot everything except being in that great, black, quiet place where nothing moved and nothing ever would—or so it seemed. Rob ought to be getting lots of colorful details for his sidebar—a desolate crisscross of railroad tracks; a pitiful thicket of neglected buildings, shabby, uninhabited, squat, full of things that would leave soon; a quiet that was thicker than blood. I almost giggled at that one, knowing Rob would die before he'd put his byline on a phrase like that. But I didn't because it would have been such a travesty to shatter the quiet.

Something else had other ideas. The quiet didn't shatter, exactly, but as we got closer to the old, corrugated metal warehouse, we heard something chipping away at it. Little shuffling sounds, the sounds of things being moved about. Rather clumsily. The sounds were coming from the back of the building.

"Wait here," said Rob, and started trotting toward the noise. I was right behind him.

As we rounded the corner, we saw a dark figure leap from a pile of stacked-up debris and take off away from us. One glance told the story; the debris—mostly boxes—was piled up under a window, which was clearly the target of an amateur burglar—who was even now disappearing around the opposite corner of the building.

"Go back, Rob," I hollered. "Head him off."

I figured that way we'd have the guy trapped—I'd be behind him and Rob could make it back to the front of the building before he could. We'd have a finger-lickin' good burglar sandwich. But Rob wouldn't play. He kept on coming behind me, and passed me in about a second, so I turned and went back to head the guy off.

Rob stopped a minute, apparently not knowing what to do, started to turn toward me, then changed his mind and started chasing the burglar again. I'm a slow runner, and Rob had just illustrated once again the sad fate of he who hesitates—the burglar was already running down the street by the time we got to the front of the building. We rounded our respective corners at about the same time, huffing, puffing, and feeling silly. At least in my case. I was also mad. We'd lost the burglar, and the way I looked at it, it was Rob's fault. I'd had a perfect plan and he'd messed it up.

But the fact that we'd lost the burglar didn't stop us. We kept chasing him, all the way to the end of the block, then into a sort of never-never land where there were a lot of railroad tracks. And a train bearing down, fast. But not too fast for the burglar to get across in front of it. For a moment, Rob looked as if he might try it, too, but I grabbed him. I didn't want him hesitating and waiting too long with a train coming at him.

We didn't speak for a moment, just tried to get our breath back while the train passed. Then Rob apparently had an idea. He couldn't tell me about it because the train was making so much noise. He just grabbed my arm and mouthed, "Come on." And led me back to the car.

"Let's wait," he said finally. "Maybe he left his car around here. As soon as the train noise dies down, it'll be completely quiet again and we can be pretty sure any car we hear is his."

I could see it was a good idea, but I wasn't about to say so. "Okay," I said grudgingly. "But I don't see why you won't listen to any of my ideas. He wouldn't have gotten away if you had."

He put a hand on the back of my neck. "I was afraid you'd get hurt."

"I'm a big girl."

He rubbed my shoulder fairly convincingly. "Look. If I'd gone back to head him off and he'd had any sense, he'd just have stopped and waited for you to run into him. Then he'd have had a hostage."

"He *didn't* have any sense. Nobody does when someone's chasing them."

"Babe, I was just—" He stopped and listened. Sure enough, someone had just started a car up. Rob's was already warmed up and ready to go, so we had a slight advantage— if we could find the other one. We slipped into Seventh Street

with our lights off, and followed the noise. Then we saw it—
on King Street, its lights just coming on. It took off.

We were right behind it, lights still off. After a zig here
and a zag there, it turned onto Third, going south, and Rob
had to hit his lights to follow. Third is the main thoroughfare
in the neighborhood and there'd be traffic. So there was no
choice but to turn the lights on. But when the burglar saw us
do it, he must have caught on to who we were, because he
floored his accelerator. We hadn't quite completed the turn
yet, so the burglar's car zoomed ahead—a piece of awful
luck, because we might have gotten his license number if
we'd been a little closer.

But Rob wasn't giving up yet. He hit the gas, too. Third
is a long, long street, and it will take you straight to Hunters
Point, San Francisco's meanest ghetto, if you let it. I wasn't
thrilled at that prospect, but it beat losing the burglar—I
wanted to get him if we had to cover the city like Steve
McQueen in *Bullitt*.

We very nearly did. Third Street has traffic lights on it,
and I guess the burglar decided he couldn't take the chance
of hitting a red one. He turned right soon, into the neighborhood at the bottom of Potrero Hill. This is much like the
area around China Basin, all warehouses and railroad tracks.
There were a million streets, and who knew where any
of them led?

The burglar, apparently. He whizzed in and out, around
and about, like a rat in a maze he's used to. We weren't used
to it, but we had a rat to follow and we were doing pretty
well when we heard a siren.

I looked behind us but couldn't see a cop. Rob turned off
his lights again and kept his eyes on the rat. Why he thought
going dark was going to help I don't know. The futility of
the whole thing suddenly came home to me.

"Rob," I said.

No answer.

"Let's give up."

Still no answer. Just a tighter set to the lips. I sat back. Oh
well, it was only halfhearted on my part anyway. I still

wanted to catch the burglar in the worst way, and my blood was still full of adrenaline. If he wanted to be macho, I'd go along with it. We were careening around on a corner on two wheels when I caught sight of a black-and-white—only a couple of blocks behind us.

Rob apparently saw it about the same time. "Omigod," he said, and gunned it again. We'd been going about sixty, a lot faster than was safe, and I hate to think how much worse it suddenly got. We needed to keep going straight for a while, because we certainly couldn't turn any corners, but the only trouble was, we couldn't go straight. In that neighborhood, you can run into things if you don't turn corners. So Rob did, somehow or other. My fingers hurt from clutching the door handle and my teeth hurt from clenching them.

The couple of turns we had to take weren't a bit smooth. In fact, we went up on the sidewalk both times and would have hit bus-stop signs, parking meters, buildings, or small children if there'd been any to hit.

I figured Rob was pretty scared and I knew I was. It had finally come home to me that we were doing about ninety on city streets and a car full of cops was chasing us. I was a lawyer and had my professional standing to think of. Not to mention my mother. I started pleading: "Rob, honey, we can't do this. My mom'll kill me."

"Shut up."

"Don't tell me to shut up. Let me out of this car right now."

Instead he turned back onto Third and once again gunned it. Now we were going about a hundred and ten. He hit the horn, and cars started falling all over themselves to get out of the way. If we didn't get in a fatal crash, my mother really was going to kill me, but the truth of the matter was, it was fun. Really a lot of fun.

I said, "Wheeeeee!" and Rob laughed.

"Hang in there, kid," he said.

I was hanging and he was laughing and we were generally having the times of our lives when we heard the crash. I looked around and saw the cop car stopped, spun around at an intersection, its back end crumpled. Another car was stopped there, too, and there was broken glass all over the street. Suddenly it wasn't fun anymore.

Rob turned off Third quickly and stopped as soon as he could. He was shaking. I felt awful. We'd done an unbelievably stupid thing and somebody might have gotten hurt on account of it. At the very least, there was property damage.

Rob said, "Think they got our license number?"

"I don't see how they could have. They were never close enough."

"So if we turn on the lights, we're just an ordinary white Toyota with two respectable citizens in it. 'Yes, Officer, we did see a crazy driver with his lights off. He went thataway.' "

"I don't think it's funny anymore."

"Hey. Neither do I. But we can either give ourselves up or we can think of a way out of this."

I didn't say anything. Rob flipped on his lights and turned onto Army Street, heading west toward the freeway. There were lots of other cars here, some of them white Toyotas. Probably this was the most sensible course. Rob had broken about a million traffic laws, had caused an accident, and might be in any amount of trouble if we turned ourselves in. On the other hand, I was an officer of the court. I myself had been an accomplice to his crimes, and now I was condoning further law breaking. What kind of hypocrite was I? How did I get into this anyway?

Suddenly I remembered how I met Rob. It was during distressing events that occurred after I agreed to help out a friend by playing the piano in a bordello. Sometimes I had lousy judgment; that was one of them, and so was this. I'd not only been Rob's accomplice, but had also enjoyed that stupid chase. If I didn't learn to curb my impulses, I was going to get disbarred.

Disbarred. Help!

"We shouldn't have done that," I said.

"You were the one who said, 'Wheeee!' "

I sighed. There was just no point in arguing, because I couldn't win—I was as guilty as he was and I knew it. I put my hand on his knee. "Sorry, pussycat," I said, "But, maybe, you know, out of respect for my job and everything, do you think we could stay within the law from now on?"

He smiled and held my hand for a minute. "I think we should try, anyway."

"Good. I want to go to bed. Could we do that next?"

"Second to next."

"Huh?"

"What would you do if you were a burglar who was interrupted on his rounds and being pursued by a carful of good guys when suddenly the police started chasing the good guys?"

"Aha! Go back and burgle away."

Rob turned onto the freeway. "So let's see if we get another crack at him."

I guess I should have said we should call the police and let them take care of it. But half an hour ago, I'd wanted to catch that burglar in the worst way, and now the feeling was coming back. I decided not to think about the cops anymore. Rob was driving the car; I'd just let him drive it.

Once again, we parked down the street and sneaked up on fog feet. It was quiet in front of the warehouse, or almost quiet. I thought I heard a faint thumping, and shushed Rob. He didn't hear it.

We'd started to go around the back when he stopped and shushed me. We stood there, silent for a long time, until both of us were sure. It was very faint, but there was a thumping coming from inside the building. An erratic thumping that wasn't coming from machinery unless it was badly malfunctioning.

"Let's call the police," I said.

Rob nodded.

But as we walked back to the front of the warehouse, I couldn't resist trying to get a look inside. There were some first-floor windows, but they were dark. I looked in them anyway, getting no reward for my trouble. Then I tried the door. It opened. Just like that, nothing to it. The thumping got loud and another sound joined it—something along the lines of "mmmmmf."

I groped along the wall for a light switch, found it, and had the place ablaze by the time Rob came in. We were in a foyer, and there was a small room to the right. The noise seemed to be coming from there. Rob pulled me back and insisted on going first—to put it another way he tried to elbow me out of the way. I elbowed back, and we ended up squeezing through the door together, which was probably a hilarious spectacle. But the guy on the floor was in no mood for a laugh riot.

He was a mild-looking middle-aged chap wearing glasses and the uniform of a security guard. He was tied up and gagged, still kicking on the floor, and making that erratic thumping noise.

We introduced ourselves while we untied him, to save him being frightened. When he could, he said his name was Larson—Larson Jones—and asked for a drink of water, which Rob got for him from a bathroom down the hall.

Larson rubbed his head when we asked what happened. "Not sure," he said. "Somebody slugged me from behind."

"In here? How'd they get in?"

He shook his head and then stopped, apparently not caring much for the way it felt. "I was outside. I make rounds every half hour."

"So somebody slugged you and dragged you in."

"I guess so. The door was locked, but the key's in my bunch." He held up the keys and started separating them. "Was. I guess he took it with him." He sighed. "I guess he got what he wanted."

"Maybe not," I said. "He probably wanted the sourdough starter. We caught him trying to break in a back window and he ran away."

Larson brightened. "You're kidding."

"No."

He smiled outright. "I'll bet the sumbitch didn't get it then." He walked out of the room and motioned for us to follow. We took an elevator to the second floor, and when we got out, we were facing a vaultlike door with a combination lock on it. "The freezer's in there," said Larson. "We just had this new lock put on." He patted it. "I couldn't tell him the combination, because he had me knocked out cold. So he painted himself into a corner." Larson laughed long and hard as he opened the door.

The room we entered was so cold it froze the hair in your nostrils. "Maybe you folks better wait out here," said Larson, but we were having none of it. We followed him through the freezer to the Martinelli chest and watched him open it. It was empty.

That seemed to disconcert Larson. He reacted by turning on us and pulling his gun. "All right, let's go. Let's get out of here."

As ordered, we preceded Larson out of the room, all the time trying to talk sense to him. "Larson, *think* for a minute. We didn't take the starter or we wouldn't be here. We untied you, we scared the burglar away, we're just nice Rebecca and nice Rob—we've even got IDs and everything. We wouldn't hurt a fly, honest."

But it was no good. Larson was freaked out good and proper. He didn't have the thief, but he did have a couple of witnesses. Or something. And as long as he was pointing the gun, he was in control. So he kept pointing it.

He got us downstairs and kept the gun on us while he used the phone in his office to call the cops. And then he still kept pointing it.

Rob looked at his watch and sighed. "Larson," he said, "remember how I told you I was a reporter? Well, I've got about half an hour to get this story in the paper. Do you think, while we're waiting, I could maybe use your phone?"

"Uh-uh."

"But what harm would it do? Really, when you think about it?"

"I ain't sure you're a reporter."

Rob started to reach in his breast pocket, where he kept his wallet. Larson raised the gun. "Hold it!"

"Hey, I was just going to show you my press card."

"You sit still. Right there." Larson waved the gun at the place where Rob should sit.

But Rob didn't sit. "Listen, Larson, old buddy, I know you've been through a scary experience and everything. I'm sorry you got bonked on the head and all, but I've got to phone my story in, and this is false imprisonment. You've got no right to hold us like this and I'm seeing my lawyer, Ms. Schwartz, about it right now."

I nodded solemnly. "That's right, Larson. I'm afraid you'll have to let us go."

"The police can let you go if they want to. I'm holding you till they get here."

Rob said, "I'm going now, Larson." He started backing out of the room, hands up like a bit player in a western.

I was horrified, and spoke before I thought. "Rob, don't!"

Larson turned to look at me for a split second, and Rob turned around and started running. He was out the door and going for his car before Larson recovered, and then Larson was standing in the door, arm raised and taking aim.

CHAPTER 12

Rob was a jerk for running out at a time like that, but he was my man and he was in hip-deep trouble. Before Larson knew what hit him, I was on his back like a monkey on a junkie's. He slammed into the left side of the doorsill just as the gun went off, and I made a grab for it. I might have got it, too, if I hadn't been sneaking a sidewise glance to see whether my sweetie was alive or dead.

Alive! Alive and nearly safe in his car.

I didn't get the gun, but the sight of Rob on his pegs was enough to give me courage to go on. I tried a karate chop on Larson's forearm, but it didn't seem to have much effect. He just looked at me, apparently trying to figure out what species I was.

Hell! Homo sapiens female, that was what. So I didn't know karate. Big deal. I could pull hair with the best of them. Right away, I started on that, and also I got Larson's glasses off and crunching under my feet, which I liked quite a lot, and I thought maybe a kick in the shin would be nice for a follow-up. But suddenly Larson remembered he was bigger than I was and had a gun. He grabbed my hair-pulling arm just as I was delivering the kick, so I had to give up on his head and torso. But I still had my legs.

I got ready for another kick, but I never got to give it. That schmuck—you're not going to believe this—kicked me first. Me, Rebecca Schwartz. A lady.

So of course there was nothing to do but nail him again,

and I still had one free hand; but so did he, and it had a gun in it. Which he smacked up against my face.

I dropped like a rose petal. Not like a lead weight or a rock. Like a petal. I just sort of floated in the breeze until the nice warm ground came up underneath, all supportive and cozy.

Now, Larson, he dropped more like a rock. Right to his knees. He set the gun down and started shaking me. "Miss Schwartz! Wake up! Miss Schwartz, are you all right? I'm not a violent man, really. I don't know what got into me. Please, Miss Schwartz, don't be dead."

I wasn't even unconscious, but I was going to let the big schlemiel suffer awhile. So I kept my eyes closed. It was a little like having that childhood revenge everyone dreams about—the one in which you die and *then* they're sorry. I just lay there with my cheek throbbing, listening to old Larson, and it was music to my ears. It was soon joined by the sound of a siren.

I flicked my eyes open. "Get up, you big oaf."

And then I was sorry I'd said it. Larson was actually crying. "Oh, Miss Schwartz, thank God. I'm a family man. I've never done anything like this."

"Just let me up."

Fear came back into his eyes. "Now, wait a minute there. I'll decide when you get up." He picked up the gun and stood up.

"I thought you were glad I'm alive."

"I still don't know if you're who you say you are. I never heard of a lawyer jumping up on somebody's back and attacking."

I hollered. I couldn't help it. "You were trying to shoot my boyfriend!" I leaped up, not even caring that he had the gun and he was threatening me. I just got up and yelled, "You goddam killer! You societal menace!" And I went for his throat.

Red lights flashed and someone spoke loudly: "Hold it right there!" Someone else said, "Drop it!"

It was the cops, of course. It was sort of disappointing to

learn that in real-life dramas, their dialogue is the same as it is on TV. However, what they said was brief and to the point. I held it right there, and Larson dropped it. Both of us even put our hands up, the result, no doubt, of brain rot caused by the tube.

I never go anywhere—even burglar-hunting—without my trusty Sportsac shoulder bag (genuine synthetic and indestructible), so I had some ID and of course Larson had his uniform. But even so we had a lot of explaining to do. Each of us, naturally, felt his or her own side of the story was the more important, and neither would shut his or her mouth and let the other one talk.

I was trying to explain that Larson had falsely imprisoned my friend and me and tried to kill my friend—who was a respectable member of the community—by discharging a firearm, and that furthermore he had pistol-whipped me for no reason at all except that I had tried to defend my own true love and myself.

Larson, as far as I could tell (I wasn't listening too well), was claiming that Rob and I were the ones who clobbered him and stole the starter, then tried to throw him off the track by coming back and untying him. But he, Larson, had seen through our nefarious plot and rounded us up for the proper authorities. Alas, he had been thwarted when I magically transformed myself into a fearsome gorgon and leaped upon his back, allowing my accomplice to escape.

I think he believed it, too. A true paranoid, that Larson. He probably thinks the CIA is in league with the Mafia, OPEC, and the DAR. He shouldn't be allowed to carry a gun. He ought to use his talent constructively, maybe start a newsletter called *Conspiracy Times* or something.

The fellows in the black-and-white apparently weren't psychologists. Or even perceptive. They didn't say, "Gee, Miss Schwartz, sorry this awful thing happened to you. We're locking this maniac up right away and we sure hope your face gets better soon."

They said, "You have the right to remain silent . . . any-

thing you say can be used against you in court . . . you have
the right to talk to a lawyer. . . .''

Stuff like that. That is no way to talk to a nice Jewish girl
from Marin County and I so informed the officers. Which, I
guess, is why I was booked for resisting arrest as well as for
assault.

I had once been picked up for drunk driving, but this was
ten times worse. A hundred times worse. Nightmare-strength
ignominy.

They actually threw me into a cell. That was bad, but it
was nothing compared to what I knew I had to go through to
get out. There you really got into your chamber-of-horrors
material. I had to make a phone call.

I actually had to call someone and say, ''This is Rebecca
Schwartz, and I'm in jail, and I wish you'd bail me out.''
O degradation! O debasement!

Who was I going to call? My mom? I could hear her already: ''I'll have to send the bail by messenger, because I'm
sitting shiva for your father. His favorite daughter has just
killed him.''

Definitely not my mom.

My dad? Isaac Schwartz, the famous criminal lawyer? I
could hear him, too: ''Beck, you're a fine lawyer, a great
little lawyer, but don't you think if you weren't so impetu-
ous . . .'' No. Not Dad either.

And certainly not Rob. I'd had time to give him some
thought, in the back of that black-and-white, and I was thinking of sending him a large bouquet of poison oak. He'd risked
his skin—and mine, when you thought about it—for some
stupid newspaper story, and not only that; he'd also put me
in the position of having to duke it out with a lunatic to save
his life and then getting tossed in jail for my pains. They'd
be wearing fur parkas in Death Valley before I'd call him for
a quick rescue.

Who else was there? Chris, of course. Why hadn't I
thought of her in the first place? I dialed. ''This is the recorded voice of Chris Nicholson,'' said her machine, and
gave message-leaving instructions. Where *could* she be? But

then what did it matter? She wasn't home and couldn't help me. "Try me at home," I told the machine. "If I'm not there, call City Prison instantly. I may still be moldering there." A bit melodramatic, but that was the kind of mood I was in.

That left Mickey. She wasn't likely to have any money lying around, but surely she could raise some. Couldn't she? Kruzick answered. "Yeah?" That was his style.

"Alan, this is your boss, and you are fired if you give me any kind of crap whatsoever at this moment."

"You on the rag or something?"

"Okay, that's it. Darken my office door ever again and you are dead as well as fired. Please tell my sister that I am currently incarcerated at City Prison and wish to hear her sweet familiar voice."

"Uh, Rebecca, listen, we had kind of a little tiff and—"

"And what?"

"Well, she went out somewhere. I don't exactly know where."

"Okay, Alan. You're back on the payroll, you momser. Just get me out of here. Fast."

"But—"

I hung up without even telling him what the bail was. Why bother? He wasn't going to get me out anyhow. Nobody was. I was going to have to stay there the rest of my life, which wouldn't be very long. I would die of exhaustion because I had to keep standing up. If I sat down on the bed in my cell, I was sure to catch something. Syphilis, probably, or worse yet, body lice. I started pacing. That must have annoyed the deputy, because she came to see what the trouble was.

"First time in?"

I nodded.

"Prostitution?"

I shook my head and swallowed. "Assault. But I didn't do it—I mean, I was just defending myself."

She nodded automatically, and I could see it was a story she heard an average of three times a day and believed every time the bay dried up. If I ever got out of there, I was going to kill Rob Burns, probably by flaying.

"Why don't you get some rest?" said the deputy.

"No. I mean I can't. . . ." I glanced at the bunk. She nodded and disappeared. When she got back, she was carrying a clean sheet.

"I know how you feel," she said, and pushed it through the bars.

You don't expect to meet someone nice in jail. It threw me off the track so thoroughly that I forgot to feel sorry for myself while I was folding the sheet and making myself a louse-free pad to sit on. By the time I got around to sitting on it, I'd exhausted gratitude, amazement, and the milk of human kindness. I started plotting revenge against Rob, and I ended up in tears.

I was still teary when the deputy came and said I was bailed out. That was the last thing I expected to hear. I hadn't really expected Kruzick to get it together that fast. I knew he'd probably manage by morning—that is, if Mickey hadn't left him permanently, as she would if she had any sense. Once she got home, wheels would turn—young Mickey certainly wasn't going to let her big sister spend the night in jail—not the *whole* night, anyway. But I figured she'd take advantage of being away from him and savor it as long as possible. Otherwise, I certainly wouldn't have been all red-eyed and undignified like I was.

They gave me my personal belongings and let me take the elevator to the first floor. Did I mention that City Prison is in the Hall of Justice, which also houses a good many courtrooms in which I had successfully argued cases for my clients? I was just glad none of them could see me then.

Mickey and Alan were waiting in the rose-marble lobby, as I'd hoped. Unfortunately, they weren't alone. Mom and Dad were there, too. As if that wasn't bad enough, Rob was just coming through the door. But even that wasn't the worst part—he had Pete Brainard with him. Pete Brainard is a *Chronicle* photographer.

It occurred to me simply to step back in the elevator and

go back to the sixth floor, where it was nice and peaceful. But Mom was on me like wrinkles on raisins before I had a chance. She'd been crying, too, and she hadn't stopped yet. She was wearing her black Bill Blass coat—mourning, I supposed—and she engulfed me in a blanket of high-quality wool. To my amazement, she didn't utter a word of reproach. Just cried and sobbed, hanging on to me.

That was a nice surprise, but a little embarrassing. I couldn't keep my mind off Pete Brainard's strobe, which was going off repeatedly.

"Mom," I said gently, "You're wrecking my suede jacket."

She let up and I fell into Daddy's arms. "Take it easy, Beck," he said. "Everything's okay."

"I wuz robbed," I said. "I didn't do anything."

"I know, baby. We'll straighten it out in the morning. You've got the best lawyer money can buy."

That made me smile. "Modest, too."

Then Mickey hugged me, and Alan gave me the "okay" sign. The camera kept clicking away.

Rob came forward, but I stepped back. "Honey, I'm so sorry," he said.

"Don't you 'honey' me. I saved your life and you left me to rot in jail."

He looked bewildered. "But what happened? I don't understand."

Mom turned on him like one of the furies. "You get away from here, Mr. Rob Burns of the *Chronicle*. Look at that bruise on her face! You did that to my daughter, you, you"— she searched for the right words—"newshawk!"

Mickey and I both giggled. It started out as a little tiny ripple of a giggle, and before we could stop it, it was a giggle fit. Mom and Dad just stood there, with the corners of their mouths turned down, looking like a couple of tragedy masks. Several times before, I'd come very close to disgracing the family, and now I finally had, and Mickey and I were yucking it up while Pete Brainard recorded the Fall of the House of Schwartz for the *Chronicle*'s half million readers.

Rob looked as if I'd punched him in the kishkas. He finally managed to speak, in a high, kind of cracked voice. "Rebecca, are you okay?"

The giggle fit blew over, and I was suddenly very mad. "Okay? Okay? No, I am not okay, you newshawk. I have been pistol-whipped, falsely arrested and thrown in a cell, where I have probably contracted a rare venereal disease, and all because you had to phone in your stupid story."

"But, Rebecca, what happened?"

That nearly sent me around the bend. "And you're *still* thinking about it. You're not worried about me; all you can think about is what's going in the final edition. Get it from your 'sources,' newshawk!"

"Rebecca, believe me—"

Dad stepped forward and took Rob's arm, his face a skyful of thunderclouds. "Rob, I think you'd just better stay out of this."

He put an arm around me, putting his body between me and Rob and Pete, protecting me from the dread press plague. Of course, the very press he now sought to save me from was one both of us manipulated shamelessly and, in Dad's case, skillfully, every chance we got. But at the moment it seemed our bitterest enemy.

Pete had fallen back, out of the line of fire, but Rob just couldn't let well enough alone. "But, Mr. Schwartz, it's my job. If there was anything I could do, you know I—"

Mom turned on him again. Her black brows came together under her perfect silver hairdo. "There's something you can do."

Rob moved back a step or three. "What?"

She pointed at Pete. "Tell him to hand over the film."

"But I—"

Pete spoke for the first time, softly. "You know he can't do that."

Even I in my weakened condition knew he couldn't do that. Mom had no right to ask.

Rob stared for a moment at the marble wall behind us. "I'm sorry," he said, and walked away. Pete followed.

"So, jailbird," said Alan. "Need a ride home?"

And Rob was the one my parents didn't like! Just because he was only half Jewish. True, Rob was a newshawk, just like Mom said, but Kruzick needed drawing and quartering if he needed air to breathe.

"You're fired," I said.

He just smiled. "See you tomorrow."

And he and Mickey left.

That meant I had to go home with Mom and Dad, which was the last thing I wanted. Mom started in before we were even out the door. "Rebecca, it's a wonder your father's heart doesn't give out, the trouble you give him. If you don't get rid of that Rob after this and find a nice doctor or something. . . . Listen, remember Marty Becker? He grew up to be a banker and nobody's landed him yet."

At the moment I was so mad at Rob I was almost willing to take a chance on Marty, but I was also unreasonably mad at Mom and Dad for being in the middle—however unwittingly—of a fight between my boyfriend and me. My head felt as if it would crack open.

"He wouldn't like me," I said. "I'm disfigured."

"Beck, he really didn't have to bring that photographer," said Dad.

I didn't think I could take much more, and I didn't like the direction in which Dad was driving.

"This isn't the way to Green Street."

"You're coming home where you belong," said Mom.

It took all my strength to speak, and when I did, I sounded as if I were about two. "Mom, please. I just need to be alone."

She didn't answer, and neither did Dad, but I think they both got the message. Dad turned right and took me to Green Street. Of course, they had to go in with me and make sure no goblins lurked in my overpriced apartment, but then they left me blessedly alone.

"Be sure," said Mom as they went out the door, "to have those clothes fumigated before you wear them again."

I'd been thinking along these lines myself, but hearing

Mom say it made me realize that I'd reverted to being the Marin County Jewish Princess I like to think I haven't been since high school. I was suddenly ashamed of imagining lice in what was probably a perfectly clean jail. There was nothing wrong with my clothes a little dry cleaning wouldn't fix.

I hung them up and stood in the shower for about half an hour, washing my hair and rewashing it, letting jail and all its real or imagined cooties run down the drain. Then I slipped into a clean white nightie.

I was feeding Durango and company when Chris called. I babbled out my tale, going heavy on the humiliation of having my folks in the middle of my fight with Rob, which was the part that now bothered me the most, and then asked her where she'd been when I needed her.

"Nowhere special." She sounded slightly sheepish. "I just went out for a drink."

"Alone? Chris, I know you feel bad about Peter, but I really think—"

She stopped me. "No, not alone. Not a flower of southern womanhood such as myself."

"Well? Who with, then?"

"Bob Tosi."

CHAPTER 13

The entire Schwartz family, rescuing its black sheep from jail, stared at me from Page One the next morning. You'd think that would have made me cross, and you'd have been right. But the mood passed when it suddenly hit me how lucky it was that Mom wasn't wearing her mink coat.

She looked just right in her well-cut black wool underneath the tear-streaked face of a mother whose child has been wronged by the very system she works every day of her life to uphold. As for me, I thought I looked rather brave, and quite nicely surrounded by supporters.

Quite a good picture, actually, and the second pleasant surprise of the morning. The first occurred when I looked in the mirror and didn't see a purple plum instead of a cheek on the right half of my face. By some miracle, I had only a minor bruise, which would hardly show at all once I called in reinforcements from the Revlon bottle.

Rob's story was accurate, if not complete. It told how he and I had surprised a burglar in the act, but it neglected to mention that we'd whirlygigged about the city at 90 MPH for half an hour after that. The average reader could easily have gotten the idea we'd found Larson tied up the very second we scared off the sourdough thief. The story went on to describe that, finding the starter missing (actually, this was the lead paragraph; he just got back to it when it came up in the narrative), Larson drawing his gun, and Rob escaping.

After that, it quoted the police as saying only that Larson

had been booked for assault and illegal use of a firearm and that I'd been booked for assault and resisting arrest.

Then, if you can believe it, it quoted me. Even though I hadn't said a single word for publication. " 'I saw Mr. Jones raise the gun to fire,' said Schwartz, 'and I tried to stop him. If that's assault, I'm guilty as hell.' "

Guilty as hell! Not only had Rob caused me to disgrace my family in front of the entire subscription list of the *Chronicle*; now he had me swearing in public as well—I'd never get another client again. I was so busy thinking up brand-new revenges, I hardly even noticed that the telephone had rung and I'd answered.

"Still mad?" said the voice of Rob Burns. I hung up.

The phone rang again, but I didn't answer. I just went into the bathroom and put on the four pounds of make-up it took to make me look respectable. Then I put on a little mascara to divert attention from the combat zone. By that time, I'd say the phone had rung maybe forty times, and it was getting to the fish. I picked it up.

"Your daily *Chronicle* is dead wrong," he said.

"You're telling *me*, you schmuck!"

"The starter isn't missing, after all."

"What?"

"I knew I could get your attention. *Still* mad?"

"As fifty hatters. State your business, please."

"Rebecca, I can't tell you how sorry I am."

I didn't answer. Not because I was trying to be mean; I just couldn't think of a thing to say.

"Okay," said Rob. "Later, maybe. I just thought you'd want to know the company moved the starter. Fail-Safe, I mean. The manager called from home this morning."

"Could you go a little slower, please?"

"That's how journalism can backfire on you, see? I mean, we saw with our own four eyes that the starter wasn't there, so of course there was no need to confirm it. But you know what? We should have realized the burglar couldn't have gotten it—he was empty-handed, remember?"

"Rob, could you get to the point?"

"Well, once the Fail-Safe folks discovered the first starter'd been taken, they naturally checked on the second one, and it was perfectly fine. But plenty of employees and other people knew there was a second warehouse and that's where it was bound to be. They figured anybody could have found that out, and sure enough, we did, and so did the burglar. So they took the precaution of secretly moving the second starter back to the original vault."

"I see."

"Listen, could we talk? How about lunch?"

"Thanks very much for calling." I hung up. I was glad to know about the starter, but so mad at Rob I had to question his motives for telling me. Maybe he was telling me because he wanted to be nice and wanted me to know, but maybe he was using the information as a bribe, to get back in my good graces. The point was, I didn't want to talk to him, and when you got right down to it, I couldn't.

I put on a brick-red dress—the closest thing I had to a spring outfit—and drove the old gray Volvo to the office, looking forward to a comforting chat with Chris. Instead, I got "Jailhouse Rock."

I kid you not. When I opened the door to my office and walked in that fine Friday morning, I heard Elvis crooning his lungs out.

Kruzick was sitting at his desk, hands folded angelically, smile beatific, eyes Mephistophelian. "You've had two phone calls," he said. "One from the United Prisoners Union and one—"

"Alan, you're dead! You are marked, you are condemned, your days are *numbered*, do you understand? I made some very nasty contacts in that jail, and I am now going to walk into my office and pick up the phone and arrange the contract you've been asking for ever since I've known you."

"What's the matter, don't you like The King? Hey, I made this tape especially for you." He did something to the little black box on his desk that caused Johnny Cash to start describing conditions in Folsom Prison.

In the old days, women fought off their attackers with their purses. Now we are professionals, and we carry the same weapons as men. I raised my briefcase.

Alan raised his arms, looking hurt. "Hey, listen Rebecca, jail's a learning experience, you know? Gives you time to contemplate your navel." He did something else to the tape and Sam Cooke shared with me what his navel had yielded: something about sound effects on a chain gang.

I slammed my office door on "gang" and deeply regretted leaving the paper at home—I wanted to scan the classifieds for a new secretary.

No appointments were scheduled that morning, as I hadn't been sure how long the divorce case was going to take to argue. As it happened, we'd wrapped it up the day before and it was under submission—in other words, we lawyers had done our parts and now it was up to the judge. So I had the morning free, unless you counted writs I ought to write, suits I ought to file, and clients I ought to reassure. But all that could wait till afternoon—I had a free morning, and my office felt like a prison (I ought to know) and it was a nice day, and I was going to go to I. Magnin and buy myself a pink outfit for spring. One cup of Alan's hideous coffee and I'd hit the trail.

But the phone rang. "Darling, how are you feeling?"

"Fine, Mom. You can hardly see my bruise."

"You should see a doctor about it."

"Do you know any single ones?" I meant it as a joke, to get her mind off the bruise, but it was a big mistake.

"Darling, I'm so glad you feel that way. That Rob is nothing but trouble."

"I was just kidding, Mom."

But she'd got her mind on what she'd got her mind on, and she couldn't hear me. "Your father and I have never felt he was good enough for our Rebecca, and I'm just sorry it took your getting chucked in jail like a street thug to make you open your eyes."

"Mom, just because he's only half-Jewish is no reason to condemn him."

What a thing to say to a Marin County liberal. "Rebecca,

how can you hurt me like that! After the way you've been raised, how could you think a thing like that could possibly enter into my feelings?"

"I don't know, Mom. It just crossed my mind there for a second."

"Well, I think you should apologize." She was crying.

"Oh, I do! Listen, I'm really sorry, Mom. Don't cry, okay? I didn't mean anything."

"Rebecca, how could you say that to me?"

"I didn't mean to, Mom. I'm sorry."

"You practically called me a bigot."

"Well, Mom, I don't think I really did, but, like I said, I'm really sorry."

"What would *make* you say a thing like that?"

"Mom, I really don't know. It was just one of those things."

"Maybe you should see a shrink."

"Good idea, Mom. I've got to go now—have to make the appointment."

"I just don't see how you could do a thing like that."

"I'm not myself, Mom. I think I have raging hormones. Oops—Alan says I've got another call."

"Give Alan my love."

I really did have another call. It was Dad. "Darling, I've got your case all worked out. Jones won't press charges against you if you won't press any against him."

"Dad, he hit me. And he fired at Rob."

"Now, darling, don't get all upset. No way is the DA going to drop the gun charge. But the other thing is like any other misdemeanor assault with no witnesses. You say one thing and Jones says another—it's not worth pursuing."

"But, Daddy, I'm the one with the bruise."

"Sometimes we just have to compromise."

I sighed. It wasn't the compromise I minded so much—it was the feeling of losing control of my life. I was nearly thirty years old, and here I was saddled with a problem secretary chosen by my mom, who was now trying to choose my boyfriends for me, and furthermore, my dad was fighting my battles. But I am nothing if not a good daughter. I resigned myself to my fate and put it out of my mind—I was going to go out and buy something pink for spring and think about it tomorrow. Like Scarlett O'Hara.

I said, "Okay, Dad. Whatever you say."

"It's really for the best, darling. Sometimes these things just happen."

"I know, Dad. I said okay. I want you to know I'm very grateful for what you've done for me."

"You don't sound very grateful."

"I'm grateful, Dad. Really."

"Beck, you got a bad blow on the head last night. Maybe you should see a doctor."

"I'll think about it. Dad. A shrink, maybe. Right now, I've got to get some coffee."

"Coffee really isn't the answer, you know."

The top of my head was going to fly off if I didn't get off the phone, but I couldn't hang up on my own father. I started counting to ten, silently.

"Beck, are you still there?"

"I'm thinking about what you said, Dad."

"That's my girl. I wish we could talk some more, but I've got a client."

"Gee, I wish we could, too, Dad. 'Bye now."

'Bye and whew! Now for that coffee and then I. Magnin. But Krurzick came in with a long white box from Podesta-Baldocchi. "Roses are red and so are Commies; stay out of bed and you won't be a mommy."

"Alan, you shouldn't have."

"Boss, oh, boss, with bruise so fine, won't you be my valentine?"

I looked at my watch, which tells the date as well as the time. It really was Valentine's Day, and I'd forgotten all about it. "Not," I said, "in a million years." And I took the box and opened it.

It contained a dozen long-stemmed white roses. "Somebody thinks you're dead," said Alan. The card said, *Couldn't find a white flag. How about these?* It was signed, *R.*

I was about to dump the whole schmeer in the circular file, but Alan was too fast for me. He took back the box and said, "I suppose you'd think it demeanin' to my masculinity to ask me to find a vase for them, but I knows my duty, Miz Boss. I sho'ly do." I think he felt guilty about the tape.

I picked up my cup and started to walk toward the coffee-pot, which was in the minuscule reception area, when the door opened for Inspectors Martinez and Curry.

"Morning, Miss Schwartz. Heard you got in a little trouble last night."

"How sweet of you to drop by. I had a nice tour of the sixth floor, thanks. I should have let you know I was coming. You could have baked a cake with a file in it."

Curry looked blank. Martinez said, "We heard you stopped a burglary in progress."

"Oh, Inspector, I should have realized—you've come to give me a medal."

"Could you just tell us what you saw, please?"

"A guy trying to break in the back window."

"You're sure it was a guy?"

"No question about it."

"Race?"

I shook my head. "Never got close enough to see."

"Height and weight?"

"Tall. Maybe a hundred eighty pounds."

"About what time was this?"

"About nine o'clock, I guess."

"Nine o'clock." He paused. "We didn't get the call from Jones until nine-forty-five."

I shrugged. "I meant nine, give or take."

"What happened between nine and nine-forty-five?"

"The moon came up, I think. Some mothers put their kids to bed, and others helped with the homework. One or two guys scored in singles bars, and, oh, I guess a lot of folks watched 'Simon and Simon.' "

Curry smiled, but Martinez quashed him with a look. "This is homicide, Miss Schwartz."

"You mean Larson died? I just beat him up a teeny-tiny little bit."

"Miss Schwartz, I'm trying to investigate a homicide and you are interfering with my investigation."

I thought of saying, "I'm trying to have a cup of coffee and go buy a pink dress, so I can forget I ever heard the word *homicide*, and you are interfering with my desire to repress just about everything I ever heard of." But I was afraid he'd tell me to go see a shrink. So I started the count-to-ten routine again, but Chris came in from court before I'd made it to three.

"Rebecca, baby, let's see your poor face." She came and examined my bruise. "Oh, you pitiful, pitiful peachblossom. It's going to turn green, I think. Maybe a little Erace."

"Chris, you remember Inspectors Martinez and Curry."

"Of course I do." She gave them her warmest smile. "Coffee, gentlemen?"

Martinez fixed me with an icepick eye. "We'll be going. See you on the sixth floor, Miss Schwartz."

Now that hurt my feelings. I guess I must have shown it, because Chris sat me down as soon as they'd left and got coffee for me. "Hard morning?"

"A living hell."

"Tell Auntie."

"Boyfriends. Parents. Secretaries. Cops. I'm going to see my shrink. Maybe you should see one, too. One minute you hate Robert Tosi and next thing, he's your valentine."

"Valentine. That's where the roses came from." Alan had stuffed them all into a vase that would have looked nice with three of them in it. "You've made up with Pigball, then."

"No. And quit trying to change the subject."

"I wasn't. Robert Tosi is certainly not my valentine. He's a loathsome sort from the nineteenth century. He asked me out for a drink, and I thought it might be educational. That's all."

"And was it?"

"Quite. He told me all about his marriage to Diddly-bop."

"Sally."

Chris nodded. "It seems the poor fool thought she was happy staying at home and knitting. Then she started working in his bakery and he thought she was happy doing that. It came as a complete surprise that she was cheating on him."

"With Peter?"

"Yes. Naturally, I asked how they'd been getting along and whether she'd ever mentioned any changes she wanted in the marriage—maybe she thought he was working too hard and they didn't have enough time together, any little things like that. He said, 'Sure, but I didn't think it meant anything.' "

"Being liberated women who wouldn't judge a person on race, sex, or previous condition of servitude, we will not say, 'Just like a man,' will we?"

"Certainly we will. Anyhow, he found out she was cheating on him with Peter, and he suddenly remembered how she used to flirt with him at parties—Bob had thought she was just being nice because Peter was his friend. Can you beat that?"

"He sounds a little on the out-to-lunch side. Why did he tell us Peter wasn't the type to get involved in a triangle?"

"He doesn't seem to count that one. He says Sally forced herself on Peter. Also, he still claims Peter dumped her. He just can't let her have anything, can't you see that? She left him for another man, but he won't even admit the guy found her attractive—she has to be a whore who stalked Peter and got her just desserts. And that's not all. He said lots of other awful things about her."

"Like what?"

"Oh, that she's a liar and you can't believe a word she says. Nothing specific—just lots of vitriol and machismo."

"I'm glad you had such a great time."

She made a face.

"What time did you go out, anyway?"

"Late. About ten. Why?"

"The burglary was around nine. When did he call you?"

"About nine-thirty."

"That's about the time Rob and I would have finished giving the burglar the scenic tour."

"So he could have been Bob." She thought a moment and then pounded the desk with her fist. "He was, dammit! He was! He was using me for an alibi."

"Maybe not. He probably just thinks you're cute."

She bronx-cheered, but the unseemly noise was drowned by the worse one of a ringing telephone. I answered before I thought.

"Peace?" said Rob.

"I need to be left alone for a while."

"No, you don't. You've been through a lot and you need plenty of garlic and basil to steady your nerves."

That caught me off guard. It sounded so exactly right I had to keep quiet for fear of saying something friendly.

"Also white wine and sourdough. Which reminds me. You know the second starter? The one we thought was stolen last night, only it turned out it really wasn't stolen?"

"Rob, get to the point."

"It's been stolen."

CHAPTER 14

We met at the Little City in North Beach, where you can get whole roasted bulbs of garlic, which you spread like anchovy paste on your sourdough, and where the pesto is not confined to the pasta. You can get it all over your salad and your antipasto and probably your hands and face if you want it there.

It was the right place for nerve-steadying herbs, but I still wasn't sure I wanted to break bread—even garlic-spread bread—with Rob. I was the first one there, and I sat at the bar instead of a table, so as not to commit myself. He came in and kissed me on the cheek. I didn't turn the other.

"So," I said, "the second starter's been stolen."

Rob nodded. "By a sinister scoundrel who snuck away scot-free."

"Don't be cute. I'm not in the mood."

"Or perhaps a sly slut speeding scurrilously sinward."

I slipped off my bar stool. "I'm going home."

He took hold of an elbow. "You can't. You're my valentine."

"Your ex-valentine."

"Okay then. You have to give back the present I gave you last year."

He had given me a little heart-shaped ceramic box that now sat on my glass-topped coffee table in lieu of the thing that used to sit there—a heavy sculpture I'd given to Rob. It had been used as a murder weapon, and I couldn't stand to have it around anymore.

Somehow, thinking about the little heart-shaped box reminded me again of how I'd met Rob and how nice he'd been to me when I was involved in a murder case—I mean, another murder case—and how much in love with him I used to be. I guessed I still was. I sat back down.

"A carafe of the house white," Rob said to the bartender.

I said, "So how did he or she do it?"

"Who?"

"The scoundrel or the slut."

"Oh. Nobody knows. It's like the last time—nobody'd even know the starter was missing if it hadn't been for the foiled attempt at the other warehouse, which prompted a check."

"Do you think our burglar did it—the one we stopped?"

Rob shrugged. "Who knows? Shall we move to a table?"

"No. Let's talk about last night."

"I said I'm sorry." He turned his blue eyes on me and rubbed a knuckle across my cheek. "Pussycat. You could have been hurt."

I looked around to see if anyone had heard the pet name. At least, he hadn't said Rosasharon, which he sometimes called me—I wasn't sure if he thought I was the Rose of Sharon and the Lily of the Valley, or if I reminded him of the Okie girl in the *Grapes of Wrath*. Nobody'd heard "pussycat," so I felt free to answer to it: "*I* could have been hurt! You nearly got shot."

"And my brave girl friend saved me. I owe my life to you, baby, and don't think I'll be forgetting it. I thought, for openers, maybe I could buy you lunch."

The wine had come and I'd drunk half a glass, but I was no less tense than I'd been all morning. "Rob, be serious."

"I don't know what to say, Rebecca." He looked forlorn. "I've apologized about ten times. What else can I possibly do?"

"Like my mom used to say when I was a kid, you're not sorry enough."

He was silent. "Look," I continued. "Was a crummy newspaper story really so important you had to risk your life and mine and get me beat up and thrown in jail for it? That's what's bugging me.''

He shrugged, seemingly at a loss. "It's my job."

''You wouldn't have gotten fired if you'd missed the home edition. Nobody would even have noticed.''

''The *Ex* would have had it first.''

''And they'd have been up a creek, wouldn't they? Because you wouldn't have talked to them, and I wouldn't have talked to them, and they'd have had about a quarter of the story, and you'd have creamed them tomorrow.''

''But it would have been *tomorrow*.''

''You're out of control, Rob.'' I turned toward the bar and took a big gulp of wine. Then I stared down at my glass, not wanting to look at him.

''Rebecca, I've had about enough from you, you goddam—you, you . . . *princess*!''

''Princess?''

''Yes, princess. JAP. I mean, that's what you *are*, but you act more like some prissy WASP than anything else.''

''Oh, great. Slurs on two ethnic groups in the same sentence. Just because you've got a foot in both camps and can't really call yourself *anything*—''

He started laughing. ''You calling me a half-breed?''

''You calling me a JAP?'' I was laughing, too.

''We're ridiculous.'' Rob was laughing so hard he had to put his head down on the bar.

''What if anyone heard us?'' I wasn't laughing as hard as he was. I had a reputation as a liberal lawyer to uphold. But it would have served me right if anyone had overheard me— I'd have been paid back for calling my own mother a bigot.

Rob couldn't pull himself together. ''I can't stand it—''

''Rob, you know what? I don't care what kind of breed you are. But you know what I can't stand about you? It's all the different colors you are. You yellow journalist! You black-and-white-and-red-all-over newshawk! You purple-prose-smith!''

He stopped laughing. ''You really mean that, don't you?''

''Yes. And I feel a lot better now.''

"You don't respect my work."

"It's not that. I do respect your work. You just get too carried away, that's all."

"I refer you, Miss Schwartz, to Tocqueville."

"Huh?"

" 'In order to enjoy the inestimable benefits that the liberty of the press ensures, it is necessary to submit to the inevitable evils that it creates.' "

"Necessary?"

Rob nodded solemnly. "Absolutely necessary."

I made up my mind. I guess I already had. "Oh well, if it's *necessary*."

"That's the spirit. Just think of me as an inevitable evil."

"How about those inestimable benefits?"

"Let's bag lunch and go to the Grand Central Baths. It'll be a great opportunity."

"For what?"

"To see me turn red all over."

And so it was. The Grand Central Baths is one of those pure-scrubbed, Japanese-style, hygienically perfect California establishments where you can not only sweat in a sauna but also soak in a hot tub, rinse in a shower, and recover on a bed in your own little hospital-clean chamber for an hour. If you wish, you can also cause loud music to play in your chamber to cover the noise of whatever else you want to do in there. We did it all, Rob and me. He's beautiful when he's red.

We were in the last stage of the adventure—recovery—when Rob said, "You take it back."

"Take what back?"

"My prose is not purple."

"You take it back about me being a JAP."

"I will not. You're demonstrably Jewish American, and you're the princess of my heart."

How was I supposed to stay mad? I thought of a way: "Okay, then. Say I'm not prissy."

"What color's my prose?"

"A leathery brown, I think. Sinewy. Tough. Lean and taut, like you."

"That's more like it. All right. You only get prissy when I act like a yellow journalist. And I'm sure I deserve it."

I sat up so fast I got dizzy. "Is that an apology?"

He touched my right breast, ever so lightly. "Rebecca, listen. I was on adrenaline last night. When I woke up this morning and realized you really could have been hurt, I reformed. I'm a changed man, honest."

"You didn't seem to be an hour ago."

Now he touched my bruised cheek. "Well, it wasn't exactly the minute I woke up. It was while we were in the sauna. Your make-up dribbled off."

"You actually sound sincere."

"I am, believe me. You know that other time you got hurt? Last year, when that creep hit you—I wanted to kill him. When you got hit, it was like me getting hit. And then this time—when I saw your bruise, it was like I'd hit you myself. And you know how that made me feel?"

I shook my head.

"Kind of yellow and purple. I'm hungry."

That was about as sweet as he ever got, but it was good enough for me—I didn't want to get diabetes or tooth decay. Civic Center Plaza was just a few blocks away, so we decided to have a picnic there, wet hair and all.

It was a gorgeous day for February. Probably there'd be more rain before winter was officially over, so we had to enjoy the good weather while we had it. That was my reasoning.

We were happily sipping white wine and munching on sourdough and salami when we got to talking about Sally. I told Rob all about how Chris thought she was a poor, downtrodden little wife-child and how Bob Tosi said she was a conniving liar and how I wasn't sure at all. I just felt sorry for her. "But she can sure bake," I said. "Have you ever had her bread?"

He shook his head.

I indicated the loaf we'd nearly demolished. "It's lots better than this."

"You know what would solve the whole problem? If Conglomerate would just buy Sally's starter, they'd have the best loaf going and they could make her rich and famous. So she wouldn't need the Martinelli starter, and neither would they. Tony Tosi wouldn't be any worse off, because Bob wouldn't have the starter, and Bob wouldn't be, because Tony wouldn't have it either."

"What about Anita?"

"I guess she's lost out."

"Sally says Conglomerate wouldn't be interested in her because she doesn't have the Martinelli name. She thinks all they're after is prestige."

"But they already have prestige. If they had Sally's starter, then *it* would be the starter of choice."

"She doesn't see it that way. She's a complicated person—she's got the best product of the bunch of them, and she doesn't trust it, because—" I stopped, unsure why. "I think," I said finally, "she doesn't really see reality. She sees only the image of a thing, rather than the thing itself."

"If you ask me, that doesn't make her any different from anyone else in this caper. You know something? None of this would have happened if we hadn't started it."

"Don't say that. It was Peter's idea."

"It was Kruzick's idea. The point is, I wrote the stories. A major newspaper said that stupid doughball was important, so that made it important."

"You're doing a lot of soul-searching today."

"Look, I know I didn't make any of this happen, but I can't help feeling responsible."

"That way lies madness. Have some more wine."

He did, and some sourdough as well. "Sally's is really better than this?"

"Lots."

"Let's go get some."

"Are you crazy? I've got work to do."

"You actually have clients coming in today?"

"No, but I've got to catch up on things."

"Now, don't be prissy, dear. It's two-thirty and we're both half-sloshed. You won't be any good to your clients and I can't do a thing for the *Chronicle*."

"What'll you tell your boss?"

He shrugged. "I'm on special."

I already knew that meant special assignment—newspaper jargon for get out of the office and don't come back till you've got a story.

"Let's go check into the Sonoma Mission Inn," he said. "It's Valentine's Day."

We stopped at his apartment for some clothes and at mine for the same thing, plus bruise camouflage and a phone call. I couldn't get Chris, so I left a message with Kruzick, knowing he'd forget to give it to her as usual.

We hadn't yet finished our bottle of wine, so we took it with us, along with a couple of paper cups. This is illegal, but I didn't want Rob to think me prissy, so I went along with it.

Over the bridge and through Marin, to Sally's place we went. This time, since it wasn't dark, we could see the vineyards. The vines in February are like squat black sculptures, and the mustard, in full, canary-colored bloom, billows about them. What with the wine and the spirit of adventure and Valentine's Day and all, my head felt billowy, too. Pleasantly billowy. I thought maybe I'd have a massage at the inn's famous spa.

We were just entering the town of Sonoma when Rob said, "Look—it's Thompson." He honked his horn but got no response.

I opened my eyes, which I admit I'd been resting, and saw a brown car going the other way, fast. Clayton Thompson was driving it, and there was another man with him. "Who's the other guy?"

"Don't know him," said Rob. "Where's Sally's bakery?"

"On the plaza, I guess. Just about everything is."

There was another bakery on the plaza—Sonoma French Bakery—and we wasted some time there before we found the authentic Plaza Bakery. It was tiny, and there seemed to be no one there. Some peculiar things were lying on the counter—a pack of matches, a can of lighter fluid, and a tiny ball of dough, all scorched.

We could see the ovens and some tables back in a light airy space behind the counter, but it didn't look as if there were any other rooms in the place.

"Sally," I called. No answer.

"There must be a bathroom," said Rob.

I called Sally again. Again, silence.

Rob said, "Let's have a look." He stepped behind the counter and gasped. "Rebecca, don't come back here."

But I was already there. Sally was lying on the floor, near enough to the counter so she was out of sight if you were on the other side of it. She had a bread knife sticking out of her chest.

"The phone," said Rob. "Call the cops."

I nodded and glanced around. At first I couldn't see a phone. But there it was, in the back of the room. Rob stood still, staring at Sally, and then he bent down and picked up her hand, feeling for a pulse, I supposed. I walked past them, on very shaky legs, to get to the phone. I picked up the receiver and started to dial O. But there was no dial tone. Impatiently, I pulled on the cord, and it hung loose in my hand. It had been cut, just like in the movies.

CHAPTER 15

"I can't do it," I said. "I can't do it." I said it the second time to help myself understand. I should call the police; the situation cried out for calling the police; but I couldn't call the police. That was all I meant, but Rob apparently read more into it.

He glanced over at me, stood up, and started walking toward me, speaking in a voice that was ever so slow and understanding, the kind you use with a person standing on a ledge twenty stories up. "Rebecca, it's all right. Everything's okay. Maybe I could call the cops instead? How would that be?"

I held the cut end of the cord up and made a face at him. Sally was dead, and somewhere inside I was sure I was upset about that, but at the moment all I felt was annoyance at Rob. My only thought was to show him I had my wits about me—I was today's woman. Today's Action Woman, able to call the cops when necessary, do whatever had to be done. I stepped past him, thinking to walk out the door and find a phone booth somewhere, not noticing I hadn't told him what I was about to do. Not even noticing that a car had just squealed to a stop outside and two uniformed cops were even now coming in the door. I bumped smack into them.

I would have fallen, but one of them grabbed my arm, and not just to steady me. "Just a minute, young lady," he said. Even in the state I was in, I was glad he hadn't said, "Not so fast." That would have put me over the edge, I think, and I would have disgraced myself with a giggle fit.

But everything was all right now, just like Rob said; the cops were there, and all I had to do was explain the situation in a calm and collected manner. Rob stole my chance. "Rob Burns of the *Chronicle*," he said.

"Oh, foot!" I blurted.

"Foot?" The cop holding my arm looked confused.

"That's what my law partner says when she's mad. She's southern, you see, and that's why she talks funny."

The cop let go of my arm and scratched his head. "*You're* a lawyer?"

Rob came over and put an arm around me. "Rebecca, I think you'd better sit down. Officer, I think you should have a look behind the counter."

The cop went for a look and I did sit down, right on the floor. Rob sat with me, either to humor me or because his legs had given out, too. The second cop stood over us, making sure we wouldn't make a break for it. She had a very pretty face, but her bullet-proof vest was more functional than flattering.

I remembered to tell her the phone cord had been cut, and then the male cop came back, pale as paper, and there was a great flurry of radioing for an ambulance and more cops.

"She's dead, isn't she?" I asked, but no one answered me. And then I said, "Thompson! Clayton Thompson!" No one answered me that time either.

The cops finally introduced themselves: Officers George Williamson and Stella Tripp. I managed to tell them about seeing Thompson on the way into town, while the ambulance arrived and then went away, its occupants unable to revive Sally. I told the cops they should pick up Thompson, better get out an all-points bulletin right away, they could probably find him before he got too far. But they wouldn't listen.

Finally, Officer Tripp could stand it no longer. "You stay here," she told her partner. "I've got something to do."

She left and came back with four cups of coffee, black, that we sipped while we waited for the coroner and more cops. Eventually, the first two took us to the police station and we told our story. The coffee had a calming effect—that and Rob's arm around me—and I was able to contribute in a coherent manner. In fact, I pretty well had to carry the narrative thread, because Rob seemed to have lost the power of speech. Somehow, this had been a lot worse than finding Peter. That time, we knew something was wrong, because Peter hadn't shown up for the auction. And somehow, the sight of that bread knife sticking out of Sally's chest was a lot more final and terrible even than the sight of blood all over Peter.

Once we were restored to near-sanity and Officers Tripp and Williamson were satisfied that we really were who we said we were, they did, per my very intelligent suggestion, put out an APB on Thompson, and even as we talked, someone came in and said the highway patrol had him.

Eventually, Officers T and W even trusted us enough to answer a couple of questions we had. They told us they'd turned up at Sally's bakery in response to an anonymous tip, and they hadn't turned on their siren, because they thought it was a nut call. Just a routine check on a nut call. Nothing ever happened in Sonoma.

Just as things were going along fine, or as fine as they get when someone's been murdered, I remembered Robert, Jr., and Today's Action Woman burst into tears. "She has a kid," I blubbered.

Officer Williamson nodded. Apparently, Sally was well known in Sonoma. "We've already checked on him. He's in San Francisco with his father."

They asked us a few more questions and then said we could go. "What about Clayton Thompson?" I asked, but the nice officers only shook their heads.

We were getting into the car when Rob suddenly came alive, like a man coming out of a coma. "My story! Jeez, my story!"

"Your what?"

"I've got to get to a phone."

The resulting story was on Page One, of course. He certainly has a nose for news, I thought, a little bitterly, and then I repented. It wasn't his fault that all this had been unleased by the Great San Francisco Sourdough Auction. I wished we could run the last few weeks backward, like a movie, and start again with all of us sitting at the Sherlock Holmes pub, talking about anything but sourdough.

Mom called, right on cue, just as my English muffin popped out of the toaster. "Your father didn't sleep a wink last night."

"I'm sorry, Mom. I'm fine, honest. Rob stayed with me."

"Rob! I thought you were done with him, and then he leads you off to some *hinterland*, where you get in more trouble."

I was buttering my muffin as we talked. Now I took a bite, and it tasted like fish food. "Gosh, Mom," I said. "I forgot to feed my fish."

And I hung up with a great rush, as if my finny pals were about to give up their collective ghost. Surely one mother would understand another's need to feed her family.

But the phone rang before I could do my maternal duty. "Listen, Mom, really—"

"It's Rob. Thompson's been released."

"He didn't do it?" I hadn't really thought about whether he'd killed Sally or not. I guess I'd just assumed he had.

"Apparently not. He found the body before we did."

"Ah. He was the anonymous tipster."

"Right. The brain's back in gear, I see."

"But why not wait for the cops? I don't get it?"

"Neither do I, but I'm hoping to find out. He's agreed to an interview."

"Today? But you don't work on Saturday."

"Dammit, I'm on special. Want to come or not?"

Of course I wanted to come.

Thompson had asked Rob to meet him, not at Rick and Mary's, but at the Stanford Court. Its lobby bar looks like a St. James Street men's club, and during the day the guests use it for business meetings. It's one of my favorite places in San Francisco—elegant without being snooty. Thompson, suited and tied even though it was Saturday, looked as if he belonged. He said, "Mornin', Rebecca. I'm glad you could join us. Once I started working again, I moved back here—the baby was keepin' me up."

I was sure Rob hadn't asked permission to bring me, or even mentioned that he intended to. Thompson was a gent, and I had a momentary pang of guilt for thinking him a murderer.

"Sit down, sit down," He gestured as if the lobby were his own living room. "Glad to see you, Mr. Burns."

We made ourselves comfortable and ordered coffee. "I guess you're wonderin' why I agreed to this interview."

Rob said nothing.

"It's just that I felt kind of stupid about what I did and I wanted to kind of explain. Sort of make a public apology." We nodded. "It was a dumb-ass thing I did—cowardly. My daddy wouldn't have been proud of me."

"Finding the body must have been pretty nerve-wracking," I said. "I know, because we did it, too."

Thompson shook his head. "You don't understand. I didn't exactly find the body."

"But I thought you phoned in the tip."

"She was still alive when I got there."

Rob took charge of the interview: "I think you'd better begin at the beginning."

"I'll be glad to, Mr. Burns. You see, I went there because it looked as if the Martinelli starter had slipped through my fingers—Conglomerate's fingers, that is. But I'd heard Miss Devereaux's sourdough was better than any other on the market, so I told the folks in New York about it."

"Your bosses?"

Thompson nodded. "They thought maybe this was a great opportunity. We could 'discover' Sally Devereaux, you know? She was a pretty gal, and we thought she might be promotable. We could have her do our TV commercials and talk about bakin' bread, and we could call our bread Sally Devereaux—it would have been like our competition, Sara Lee, only Sally was a real person."

My stomach turned over as I realized how much Sally

would have loved that. If she'd lived a few minutes longer—maybe only a few seconds—she might have had the kind of success she never even had the nerve to wish for.

"So, anyway," continued Thompson, "I went up to Sonoma to taste her bread and talk with her. I didn't make an appointment—didn't want to get her hopes up until after I was sure the bread was really as good as folks said it was.

"When I got there, I didn't see anyone in the place. But there was a funny smell, like somethin' was burnin'. And there was somethin' that looked like a burned ball of dough on the counter."

"We saw it, too. Along with some lighter fluid and matches."

"Yes. I could still smell the burned smell, so it seemed as if someone had been there pretty recently. I thought they still were—in another room or a bathroom, maybe. I was still tryin' to get my bearin's when I heard a moan. So I stepped behind the counter and"—he turned up his palms in a helpless gesture—"there she was."

"What did you do next?"

"I bent down over her. She had that big knife stickin' out of her, so I knew I had to get help right away, but—I don't know, your first instinct somehow isn't to go to the phone first thing. So I bent down and she took my hand. I don't know if she knew who I was or not; maybe she didn't care. She just knew I was a person. She told me she had to go to the bathroom." His eyes filled up and so did mine. There she was dying with a knife in her chest and her last conscious thought was that she had to go to the bathroom. It didn't seem fair.

"Did she say anything else?"

"Yes." An odd look came over Thompson's face. "She said she needed a gun."

"A gun!"

"Strange, isn't it? I think she wanted to kill the person who stabbed her. She didn't say that, though. She just said she needed a gun and a bathroom. Oh, and she mentioned Peter's name, too."

"In what context?"

Thompson shook his head, looking very sad. "None. She just said his name and then she died. I was so shook up all I could do was get out of there. I got in my car and started drivin'."

"You're sure she was dead?"

If Thompson sometimes struck me as a bit of a wimp, he didn't then. His eyes were marble-hard. "*Dead* sure, Mr. Burns. Her hand came out of my hand, and her breath left her. It wasn't something you could mistake."

"I'm sorry, Mr. Thompson. Did you phone the police before you got in your car?"

"Nope. Didn't even think of it till I was a good ways down the road."

"If you were calm enough to call the cops, why didn't you just give them your name and come clean?"

"Could I answer that off the record?"

Rob hated those last words. He twitched a little, but he nodded.

"Well, I was still panicked, but I knew I'd better call the police. I mean, I was raised right and I knew I had to. But, frankly, I didn't see any reason in hell for gettin' involved. The murder wasn't my fault, I didn't know one thing that could possibly shed any light on anything whatsoever, so why not take advantage of the situation I was in—away from the scene of the crime, I mean—and keep on stayin' away?" He smiled the smile of a man who knows he has acted in a wholly human, if not wholly admirable, way. "I didn't know y'all were going to spot me."

"The police told you we were the ones who saw you?"

"No. I guessed. All I had to do was read the *Chronicle* and put two and two together."

"That brings up something I've been wondering about," said Rob. "Who was the guy in the car with you?"

"I don't know what you mean, Mr. Burns. There was no one in the car with me."

"Rebecca, didn't you see someone with Mr. Thompson?"

"I did, yes."

"And so did I."

Thompson looked as if his kid were trying to tell him an heirloom vase had sprouted legs, jumped off the mantel, and busted itself. "I can't think what you two are talking about. You can ask the highway patrol if you don't believe me."

CHAPTER 16

That creep Rob left me again—well, he let me buy him lunch and then he left me—something about getting his story written—and I felt strangely at odds. I was unhappy and didn't want to be alone. I decided to visit my sister.

Mickey and my ace secretary lived in the Noe Valley now, in one of those Very San Francisco apartments with big rooms, high ceilings, and two bathrooms—one for the toilet and one for the tub. Since they'd both started working, they'd replaced some of their Goodwill furniture with new stuff from Macy's, and the place looked close to presentable. It might stay that way this time—Mickey's gotten a wicker sofa her cat can't shred.

Kruzick answered the door. "No," he said. "Absolutely not. No floors, no windows, no weekends. Find a Kelly boy."

As usual, I just wasn't in the mood, but I must have been even less so than usual—even Alan noticed. "Oh, all right," he said, waving me inside, "I guess I could make you some coffee, since you love it so much when I do." He shook a finger at me. "But no dictation; not in your lap, anyway."

Mickey turned off the vacuum and came running to kiss me. "What a great excuse not to clean house."

Alan grabbed a dust rag, which looked strangely alien in his grasp. "I have to do everything around here."

Mickey rolled her eyes and went to make the coffee he'd promised.

While I waited on the new wicker couch, I curled up with Lulu the cat, thinking about Sally. When Mickey got back,

I filled her in on the few details of my recent activities that hadn't been reported in the *Chronicle*.

"Let's think," she said. "Why would anyone want to kill Sally?"

"Let's do indeed. Somehow, I just assumed Clayton Thompson had done it until the cops let him go."

"Thompson?" Alan stopped pretending to dust and looked around. "That redneck who came to the auction?"

"He's no more a redneck than Chris is—he's just southern."

"He came to the play the other night. With a cute boy."

"Aha!" said Mickey. I was kicking myself too hard to answer. Of course Thompson was gay. That was why he'd been staying in the Castro, and why he claimed there'd been no young man in his car, and why he was so nervous the day of the auction. I remembered trying to make small talk with him that day. He'd even acted twitchy when we asked him about sightseeing, and now I knew why—the sights he'd seen were confined to Castro Street. He had a wife and kids and he was southern, even if he did live in New York—he couldn't afford to come out of the closet. But he was no doubt making the most of every second in San Francisco, the homosexual capital of the world—or of the West, anyway.

And of course he'd gone to see *Sleuth*. He knew all about it from reading Rob's articles on Peter, but they didn't say Alan was in the play, so he didn't know he could blow his cover there. Had Peter known him before? It seemed impossible—how could he have?

Mickey ran a hand through her unaccustomed short curls. The hairdo was as new as the sofa, yet another sign of her urbanization. Her mind returned to the original subject. "Just because the police let him go doesn't mean he didn't kill Sally. Maybe he saw you on your way to Sonoma, figured you'd tell the cops he'd been there, and made the phone call so he'd look clean."

"Oy." Why hadn't I thought of that?

"Maybe he did it," she continued, "because he was the burglar and Sally found out about it."

"Why else do it?" I said, thinking aloud. "Why would anyone kill Sally? I just don't get it."

"Maybe the murder hasn't got anything to do with sourdough," said Mickey. "Maybe her boyfriend did it."

"Or maybe Bob Tosi did it—maybe he never got over her leaving him for Peter, which would also argue that he killed Peter and made both crimes look like sourdough murders. Or maybe he did it because he wants custody of the kid."

"I like it," said Mickey. "He's the only one who hasn't seemed very interested in getting the starter—no one would ever suspect."

"It won't work—he's got a great alibi."

"What?"

"The kid. Sally's own kid."

"Maybe not." She looked very excited. "It takes an hour to drive from here to Sonoma, right?"

I nodded.

"Well, how long is it by bus?"

"I don't know. Why?"

"Because that must be how she sent the kid—and the bus must take at least an hour, probably longer. So, look—here's what he does: He knows he's supposed to pick up the kid at, say, four. Does that sound right?"

I nodded.

"So he drives to Sonoma, watches Sally put little Bobby on the bus, follows her back to the bakery, stabs her, and drives home in time to pick up the kid. He might have to speed a little, but I doubt it—the bus probably takes an hour and a half."

"I don't like it."

"What do you mean, you don't like it? Are you kidding? It's perfect. It's like the *Five Red Herrings*."

"Oh, the timing's perfect, all right. And the brilliance of the theory is dazzling. But you don't know Bob Tosi."

"I thought you said he was a jerk."

"He's arrogant, anyway. But he's sane."

"What do you mean? He's used to getting everything he wants. He's probably a spoiled brat who'll do anything to keep it that way."

I shook my head. "He's gotten a lot of things, but they've been handed to him. The truth is, he's had an easy life and he hasn't had to scratch to get ahead. I don't think he's very competitive." I stood up. "But I'm going to see him, anyway."

"How come?"

"You gave me a great idea. I'm going to find out who Sally's boyfriend is."

The idea I had wasn't exactly pretty, I'm afraid. Bluntly speaking, it involved the exploitation of a small child. But the point was to catch his mom's murderer, I told myself. Yes, Rebecca, but that's the job of the police, my conscience told me.

That did it. Could I entrust an important job like this to the likes of Martinez and Curry? Certainly not. I looked up Bob Tosi in the phone book.

He lived in Grosvenor Tower, in my opinion a weird choice for a person with choices. It was a very pricey place, indeed, with saunas and other amenities—but impersonal? Like a Holiday Inn. The apartments I'd visited there looked as if they were occupied by people in transition—just divorced and about to get engaged. Come to think of it, Bob Tosi might fit that category. He was certainly recently divorced, and from all accounts, including his own, he didn't seem the sort who gave matrimony a lot of thought before taking it on.

However, contrary to my expectations, he'd given his apartment a lot of thought. Or at least he'd given thought to his own comfort. Like his office, the place wasn't "decorated," but it was full of things that looked used and enjoyed—things like books and records, a chess game on a coffee table, and a few of little Bobby's toys. On the walls, which had been painted a friendly forest green, hung good pictures like the ones at his office—another Mary Robertson, paintings by other California artists, and a Haitian primitive, a jungle scene that seemed to dominate the room.

Bobby was sitting on the floor, untangling a kite string that was seriously snarled.

Bob greeted me—oddly, I thought—with a hug, and invited me in without question. He sat on the floor next to

Bobby and started to help him with some of the worst tangles. "This is Miss Schwartz," he said.

Bobby looked up: "Hi, Rebecca."

I said to Bob, "We met when Chris and I went up to Sonoma." And then I addressed them both: "How're you two doing?"

Bobby didn't look up at that. "Okay," he said, in a voice that belied it.

"We're having a hard time," said Bob. "We're glad to see you." The look he gave me was almost pleading—he would have been glad to see the Creature from the Black Lagoon, anything to distract him from his son's grief. I wondered if he had his own grief as well, and he answered the unspoken question: "It's hard for us without Sally. I didn't think it would be this hard."

"If there's anything I can do—"

He waved a hand, cutting me off. "We just have to live through it. We went out and flew Bobby's kite, and that helped, didn't it, kid?"

"I guess so." Bobby still kept his eyes on the floor. "I just wish I hadn't come here, that's all."

Bob's pain showed in his face. "You couldn't have done anything, son."

"I wish I hadn't been on that bus."

"Bus?"

"Somebody killed her while I was on the bus. I figured it out."

"You couldn't have known that would happen."

"I could have stopped it."

"Bobby, lots of people who were close to your mother wish they could have stopped it. It's not your fault."

Tears started to run down his face, and Bob reached for him, to hug him, but he pulled away. "I'm the only one. Nobody else was around. And I wasn't around when I should have been."

"Her boyfriend couldn't stop it," I said, hating myself.

Bobby looked up at me now, hope struggling through the tears. "Boyfriend?"

"If anyone could have, he could have. And he would have wanted to as much as you do."

"And so would I," said Bob fervently.

But Bobby ignored him; perhaps he didn't believe him. "Did my mom have a boyfriend?"

"Of course she did. You know him, don't you?"

He shook his head, apparently puzzled. "She had a boyfriend once. Right after we left here, Dad. But that was a long time ago." The tears came more freely. "And now he's dead, too. Will we all die, Daddy?"

Bob reached for him again and this time, sobbing, the boy melted into his dad's embrace. "Of course not, Bobby. Of course not. We're going to be all right. It's all going to be okay."

"You sure?"

"Of course I'm sure."

While this was going on, I felt like a nematode. A drunken, derelict, tramp of a nematode, shunned, and rightly so, by all decent nematodes. Bob, apparently, was too much in shock to notice what I was doing. If he'd figured it out, he'd probably have booted me out by then. I hated myself, but I was in too deep to stop. "Your mom's boyfriend is still alive," I said. "Don't you know who I mean? The guy who was backing her in the sourdough auction. You must know him."

Unaccountably, Bobby started laughing. "She didn't have any boyfriend. Did Mom say that?"

I didn't answer, not sure at all what was going on. "Mom was like that. She liked people to think things sometimes that weren't true. She didn't have any boyfriend, Rebecca. No one could have helped her but me."

I saw the truth of what he was saying. Sally had been a great one for appearances, and appearing desirable was important to her. There hadn't been any backer at all. She hadn't a prayer of winning the auction. Or maybe she thought she could bid high and then find a backer to make good on the bid if she won. Her fantasies had just gotten away with her. I felt like a very stupid nematode.

"Bobby," I said, "I'm sure your mom would have been proud of you for being so brave about wanting to save her." I stood up. "You're a good boy."

Bob said, "I'll walk you to the elevator."

When we were in the corridor, he thanked me for trying to make Bobby feel better, and I thanked the God of Moses and Abraham for somehow keeping my real motives from him.

"I know this is terribly hard on you," I said. "I just can't think—"

I stopped myself, but Bob urged me on: "You can't think what?"

"I can't imagine who'd want to kill her."

"Me for one."

"But you seem to be taking this nearly as hard as Bobby."

He shrugged. "Part of that is on Bobby's account. I feel like what happens to that kid happens to me. You know what I mean?"

I nodded.

"But I used to think I wanted to kill her. If I'd known it would hurt this bad when she died—on my own account, I mean, not just Bobby's—I'd have, I don't know, gone to confession or something."

"Is it too late?"

He laughed at my ignorance. "No. Maybe I'll do it. It may help."

I left, feeling dirty and debased and defeated. I hoped I would think twice the next time I decided to try to pump a child who'd just lost his mother. But I couldn't help thinking how odd it was, what Bob had said—it was almost exactly what Anita had said about Peter. Here were two families, it seemed, in which everyone thought he wanted to kill everyone else, but in some perverse way they all loved each other. Except the one who'd done a couple of them in.

CHAPTER 17

Back in the Volvo, I found my thoughts returning to Clayton Thompson. After all, he wasn't a member of the family. And he apparently had something to hide. A person with a secret is dangerous, particularly when there's a lot at stake.

I considered again the question of whether he could have known Peter before the Great Sourdough Starter Auction. Maybe he'd had other business trips to San Francisco and they'd met and been lovers. And maybe he'd killed Peter in some kind of ex-lover's quarrel, and Sally'd found out about it, so he'd killed her.

There was something wrong with it, though. Sally'd been killed with her own bread knife. If you drove all the way to Sonoma to kill someone, wouldn't you take an appropriate weapon? And what about that little still life on her counter. Lighter Fluid, Matches, and Burned Doughball. What was that all about?

I wanted to ask Thompson some more questions, but I wasn't quite sure how to phrase them. "By the way, Clayton, did you happen to kill your lover or possibly ex-lover, and also Sally Devereaux?" That wasn't going to get it. I needed an excuse—something I could use as a reason for my visit; then I could segue neatly into the matter of homosexual love and death.

Putting the brain in gear, I went quickly over our conversation that morning—was there something there I could use? There was. Indeed, there was. By the time I got to Nob Hill, I'd half-convinced myself the answer was vital. Why hadn't

I asked about it that morning? It was Rob's interview, not mine—that was why. But now Today's Action Woman was going to get some answers. Maybe I could even say, "Look, Clayton, baby, I want answers and I want 'em now." I could Bogart the whole phrase, maybe, twisting up the old lip, and I could stand all casual with one hand in my pocket.

But then I saw what was wrong with that picture; I'd turned Today's Action Woman into a man. I looked lousy in a suit and tie. I pulled into the hotel's porte cochere, reminding myself to read more Sharon McCone mysteries so I could get my fantasies right.

I asked for Thompson on the house phone. He wasn't registered, but I was undaunted. I simply drove to Rick and Mary's and rang the doorbell. Someone inside pushed the buzzer that let me in. Upstairs, Clayton Thompson answered the door with a wide smile. Which faded as soon as he saw who'd come to call: "Rebecca. I was expecting someone else."

"May I come in?"

"Of course." He didn't speak enthusiastically, but he stepped aside to let me in. If anyone named Mary lived there, my name was Susie Creamcheese. There wasn't any lavender in the place, but there were a lot more antiques, fussy bric-a-brac, and copies of weightlifting magazines than a woman with a baby needed. Not to mention pictures of strapping young men on fishing trips, playing volleyball, clowning at parties, posing with arms around each others' shoulders.

I was sure Clayton shared my opinion of his friend's taste. The look on his face confirmed it, but he seemed determined to bluff, maybe figuring I'd be too polite to suggest a decorating course for the kid. "Sit down."

I sat on one end of a peach velvet sofa, and he sat at the other end. "I've been thinking about what you said this morning—about Sally. It seemed so horrible—so sort of mundane and worthless—to live your life and then die wanting to go to the bathroom."

Thompson smiled a stingy smile. "It's not so much the needin' to. It's the havin' nothing else to say."

"Exactly. It bothered me."

He said nothing, just glanced toward the door.

"It's been nagging at me all day."

"What can I do for you, Rebecca?" His voice said his patience was fish-scale thin.

"I need to know what she said."

"But I told you. I'm afraid I don't get this at all."

"I mean exactly what she said. Verbatim."

"I told you. She said she wanted to go to the bathroom and she wanted a gun."

"I thought she mentioned Peter's name as well."

"She did." His voice was outright cold now. He wanted me to get out of there.

"But what *exactly* did she say?"

"She said Peter's name. That's all."

"Just Peter? Or Peter Martinelli?"

"Just Peter."

"Ah. And did she say that first or last?"

"I really don't see what difference it makes." The voice was high-pitched and strained, teetering on outrage.

"Well, if she said it first, it might mean she'd mistaken you for Peter."

"Really, Rebecca. She knew Peter was dead."

"But she may have been out of her head."

"Then what difference could that possibly make?"

Thank heaven he cut it off there. If he'd said, "What difference could it possibly make what she said?" thus supplying the third line of a rhyming triplet, I don't think I could have stood it.

I figured he was being such a putz because his friend was coming back any second and if I saw him, the game was up. "How long," I said on impulse, "had you known Peter before he died?"

"I beg your pardon?" He looked genuinely bewildered.

"Forget it. Let's go back to Sally."

"Very well." Deep, resigned sigh. "She said 'Peter' first."

"I see. 'Peter, I want to go to the bathroom'? Is that what she said?"

He glanced at his watch. "I've got a lot of things to do, Rebecca."

This time I said nothing. I tried to make my silence as stony as possible.

He spoke at last. "She said 'Peter.' And then she paused. In a minute or two she asked for a gun."

"A minute or two?"

"A few seconds, Counselor. Really, why don't you try a rubber hose?"

"So she really said, 'Peter . . .' pause, 'give me a gun.' "

"No, no, no. She said, 'I *need* a gun. I *need* a gun.' Need, Rebecca, *need*."

"I think I'm getting the message. She said it twice then?"

"No, no. *I* said it twice. For emphasis."

"And did you ask her why she needed a gun?"

"Of course." He shrugged. "She didn't seem to hear me. She paused again for a long time and that's when she said she needed a bathroom. And then she died, Rebecca. 'Bathroom' was her last word. Are you happy now?"

"Indeed I'm not, Clayton." I got up, not even needing, as Sally might have said, to simulate a snit. "I could care less what consenting adults do in private. You have no cause to be rude to me."

I started to walk haughtily toward the door, thinking how much more effective three-inch heels would have been than Reeboks. But Thompson caught my wrist as I tried to sail past him, seized it in a most ungentlemanly fashion. "As southerners say," I said, "unhand me, sir."

He looked at his right hand on my wrist as if it had just withered and turned black. "I'm sorry." He croaked out the words. "So terribly sorry." And then he did unhand me, uncurling the fingers slowly, giving the impression he'd just acquired them and they weren't quite user-friendly. He sat down on the couch, looking pale. "My God, it's come to this."

"You got a little excited and grabbed me. No big deal."

"I've never raised my hand to a woman before."

"Clayton, will you please lighten up? In the first place, you didn't raise your hand to me, and in the second, you did raise your voice, and you've been consistently rude to me ever since I got here. I'd much rather hear you apologize for that."

"I *am* sorry, Rebecca. Deeply sorry. I've been . . . nervous lately."

I sat down, close enough to be comforting but still a respectful distance from him. I spoke softly: "You know, in San Francisco, it's no big deal to be gay."

When I uttered the forbidden word, he seemed to shrink away from me, literally to move backward, though he really didn't budge. It was as if his whole body somehow winced. I wanted to touch him, to reassure him, but touching didn't seem to be what he wanted.

"I was so afraid you'd come in here the other night . . . that you'd see Ricky. That's why I pulled that thing about a gun. Listen, I want you to know somethin'. I paid for the smashed window at the bar, and I paid all the medical bills for the guy who got his jaw broken. That was a terrible, terrible thing I did."

"Chris and I would have been discreet. It's no one's business but yours."

"You won't tell anyone?"

"Of course not. But Rob already suspects, I guess. We both saw you with your friend the other day, and in this neck of the woods, two guys together usually means romance."

He sighed. "Ricky is my first—uh, man. I always knew I was different, but I never had the courage to act on it before. We were going to the Sonoma Mission Inn for the weekend— to celebrate our first week together."

"You mean you weren't sent to check out Sally's bread?"

"Oh, that was true, all right. We were just combinin' business with pleasure. I dropped Ricky off and went to see her. And found her dying."

"So you didn't call the cops because of Ricky. You panicked and just wanted out."

He nodded. "I went back and picked him up and we high-tailed it. We did see you on the way in, so I dropped Ricky off and told him to call the police. I figured you'd spill the beans and I'd feel a damn sight better if I were alone when the highway patrol stopped me."

"That's what we thought happened—Rob and me." I got up again. "I am genuinely sorry to have bothered you, Clayton."

"Just one thing, Rebecca."

"Yes?"

"Exactly what *was* your reason for droppin' by?"

For the second time that day, I felt like something from one of the least distinguished phyla. "I don't really know, Clayton."

The blue eyes flashed. "I beg your pardon?"

"I felt," I said weakly, "that we needed to talk."

"I understand." He nodded as if he did.

CHAPTER 18

When I got home, Rob's voice spoke to me from my trusty answering machine: "I've had it—let's go camping, and I don't mean on Castro Street."

I wasn't in the mood for gay jokes, but there was nothing wrong with the basic idea. I called back. "I've got my jeans on."

"I'll be right over."

We could only go for one night, as we both had to work Monday morning, so we decided to drive to Samuel P. Taylor State Park, a secluded redwood retreat only fifteen miles west of San Rafael, where my parents live. Usually it's pretty booked up, but we needed to get away so badly we figured we'd get lucky, and we did. Somebody with a sick kid had just abandoned a prime campsite.

Camping is something all Californians do—in the Golden State, the smallest child can build a campfire. Rob is from the East, so I'd had to teach him the gentle art, but he was getting to be quite a woodsman, which is to say he could grill a mean steak on any campfire I could whip up. And eat the steaks he grilled was about all we did that weekend. That and hike a little. And think. Or at least I thought. I found walking through groves of redwoods and madrones quite conducive to thinking. The only problem was, I kept thinking about the murders.

Motives were on my mind. Bob might have one, if Mickey were right, but if he'd killed Sally, he certainly put on a good bereaved ex-husband act. I couldn't think of a motive for

Tony, except the obvious one of getting the starter, but I didn't see how doing Sally in was going to accomplish that. The same went for Anita.

Clayton Thompson was something else again. He had lots of motives. Perhaps he'd once been Peter's lover and they'd quarreled. Or maybe he'd actually offered to buy Sally's starter and she either refused to sell it to him or held him up for more money than the company would pay, and he'd killed her to save his job. Or perhaps she knew about him and Peter, if indeed they'd been an item, because Peter and Sally certainly had, and lots of secrets come out in pillow talk. Maybe she tried to blackmail him and he figured, What was one more corpse?

All pretty fantastic, but Clayton Thompson stuck in my mind. He stayed there until I caught on to the reason for it. And once I got hold of that, I started to evolve a little theory. The only problem was, it had a few holes in it. So I decided to let it wait until Monday.

Rob and I got back to the city early Sunday evening, and he dropped me off at my place. We usually didn't spend Sunday night together, but I could have used him that night. I came home to yet another corpse—Durango's. Sadly, I fished the little guy out of the aquarium, wrapped him in aluminum foil and gave him a decent burial down the garbage chute, vowing never to get another seahorse no matter what. They just took your love and broke your heart.

I played the piano a long time to cheer myself up before I went to bed, but it didn't work. I cried myself to sleep, and not only on Durango's account. I was upset about that little theory of mine.

But I had to know. The next morning I should have made three phone calls, but I only made one. To Rob, asking him to find something out from the Department of Motor Vehicles. He said he'd get back to me. That was just as well, as I had clients coming in all morning. By the time he called back, I had seen an accused dope dealer (my least favorite kind of client) and two alleged embezzlers. You meet some nice people in my business.

Rob told me what I needed to know—Tony Tosi's license number—and I took off for the Palermo Bakery, where I found Tony sitting in an office as "sophisticated" as his brother's was naive. All impersonal tans and blacks. Tony had on a suit to match, and for that matter so did I—my best black gabardine. If I didn't get to I. Magnin soon, people would think I was in permanent mourning.

"Ah, Rebecca," said Palermo's president. "Come for that tour?" He glanced at his Rolex. "I wish you'd called—I've got a two-thirty."

"It's okay, Tony. I just dropped in for a minute."

"Don't worry, I'll put him off." And before I could stop him, he picked up his telephone and gave orders.

"Let's start on this floor, shall we? It's backwards in the process, but it's more exciting because the best part's upstairs."

If Tony's office was a bit overdecorated, it was the only thing in the bakery that was. The place looked as if it hadn't changed for fifty years, even though it was eight or ten years old. Tony had brought up a lot of ancient machines and equipment and installed the whole operation in an old warehouse.

We went out back first. "This is the loading dock. The trucks back up here 'round the clock to pick up merchandise." We stepped back inside.

"And this is our warehouse." It was just a big room full of red plastic trays with bread on them, not arranged in neat military rows, just standing around willy-nilly. Overhead, rows and rows of wire racks used as coolers moved in a circle around the ceiling. "The coolers are for steak rolls and things that will go into poly bags. The sourdough loaves that go out to the stores and restaurants are bagged hot."

He took me into another room with two lazy Susans on it. Hot loaves were dropping onto the moving tables, and ladies in white uniforms were putting them in paper bags, then into cardboard boxes for loading onto the trucks.

We went into another room, about the size of a whole city block, and walked all the way through it. At the far end, balls of dough were coming off "proofers," conveyor belts that brought them down from the second floor, very slowly. "It takes them about fifteen, maybe eighteen minutes to get to the molders," Tony explained. "They need the time so the dough will stretch easier. We call that one 'the cage.' " He pointed to an ingenious vertical arrangement of conveyors.

"It looks scary."

He shivered. "Wait'll you see the mixer." After being molded into loaves by the ancient machines, the bread was put on cotton cloths in racks called boxes, which in turn were rolled into "steam boxes" to "proof up," or rise. Tony pulled back a metal door and we went into a steam box—I could see how it got its name.

"It's about a hundred degrees in here. Hey, Lorenzo." A man in a white outfit entered the steam box, and Tony spoke to him in Italian. He turned to me. "I told him the loaves looked a little small. Anyway, it takes them several hours to proof up. Then we bake them."

He took me over to the oven, where one of the bakers was using a loaf-size board to lift the bread off its cotton cloth and put it on a "peel board," a larger wooden one that held several loaves. The loaves were then peeled—dumped—in neat rows onto the first of thirty-six shelves on which they baked. "The bread goes from shelf to shelf," said Tony, "changing shelves every fifty seconds. We bake them thirty-five to forty minutes at 435 degrees. Now let's go see the good stuff."

There was no elevator to the second floor—only an old-fashioned narrow metal staircase. The room at the top was unbelievably light and airy, and piled here and there with bags of salt, sugar, and other ingredients. The effect was rather like a huge potting shed with a good supply of fertilizer and perlite stacked in hundred-pound bags.

On our way to the room with the mixer, we passed a metal trough about twelve feet long and divided into thirds. One of the compartments was filled with dough. "That's it," said

Tony. "That's the sponge." He plunged a fist into it and so did I. It felt wonderful.

"There's lots more of those." In the next room, there were six or eight troughs, each about twelve feet long, and most weren't divided, so a hunk of dough about the size of a couple of large men could repose in each one. I was in heaven.

"They're going to mix a batch now. But first, look over there—those are dividers." The dividers were machines into which hunks of dough were being fed and cut into the round balls I'd seen on the first floor.

"Feel anything?" asked Tony.

"I think it's an earthquake." The floor was moving beneath my feet. A repeated loud thudding was going on in the mixer. The machine itself shook like a berserk washing machine. A little sign on it identified it as a product of the Triumph Company of Cincinnati, Ohio. I hoped the Triumph folks had done proper road tests; I was pretty sure the thing was about to fly apart. "Watch now. They're going to take the dough out."

A baker opened the mixer and the shaking stopped. Hunks of dough as big as loaves splattered over the outside of the thing. Inside, a mean-looking blade slowed and a mammoth wad of dough dropped into a trough set below the mixer door.

"Here goes the new batch." The mixer had two compartments, like a stove with two ovens. The same baker opened the other door, and I saw that the second compartment had flour in it. Two men cut a troughful of dough into armfuls and shoved them in, letting them deflate like balloons. Then they closed up the mixer and the shaking and thudding began again.

"Very impressive," I said. "And where do you put in the secret ingredient?"

Tony led me into another room, with nothing in it but troughs, most empty, but some delectably full. "It's a secret, of course."

I let him have it. "I know where it is, Tony. It's in the

sponge, isn't it? It's been there a long time—ever since you stole the Martinelli starter.''

"What are you talking about?''

"I got your license number the night you stole the control batch.'' I paused a moment for effect and then recited the number Rob had gotten for me that morning. "Five One Five WIN.''

I was watching his eyes, not his hands. So imagine my surprise when I felt something hit my chest and then I sank down, down, deliciously down onto a twelve-foot pillow of sourdough. The dough was wonderfully fragrant as it closed over my face.

I admit it felt good, being in there. I even admit I'd had a brief fantasy of throwing myself into one of the troughs. But I'd never have done it in my best black suit.

And not if I'd known I wouldn't be able to breathe. I had to get the dough off my face. I raised my arms, and pulled at it, but the more dough I pulled off, the more slid back on. I opened my mouth to yell—and got a mouthful of dough. I started to cough, then panicked, clawing at my face.

And then I felt someone lifting me out. When I was righted, standing goo-covered in goo-covered shoes, my rescuer was still holding on to my arms—and a good thing, too, as otherwise I believe I'd have slugged Tony Tosi. The Good Samaritan was a baker, who looked quizzically at Tony, then at me, and walked away as if whatever happened next wasn't any of his business.

When I'd gotten done coughing and looked at Tony, the urge to slug him left me. His eyes weren't wild, as I'd imagined they would be, but infinitely sad. "I . . . don't know what to say,'' he muttered. "I just lost control.''

An elderly woman, crooning in Italian, led me to a bathroom with a shower.

My hair dripping, wearing the white uniform of a lady baker twice my size, I marched back into Tony's office and threw my ruined suit on his knee-deep tan rug. I was furious about that suit.

"I didn't do it," he said, before I had time to voice the eight or nine unpleasant things I had on my mind. Things like criminal charges, civil suits, dough-covered suits, possible injury and ruined dignity.

"What do you mean you didn't do it, you schmuck? I suppose you nearly killed me to show how wrong I was."

"Okay, okay. Calm down." He raised the hand with the Rolex on the wrist, not looking as if he expected results. But I let him talk. "Look, I took the starter a couple of years ago, all right?"

I sat down, mollified.

"But I didn't take the second batch."

"I saw you, Tony. Remember?"

"That's what I'm trying to tell you. You saw me at the warehouse in China Basin."

"Then what are we arguing about?"

He shrugged, as if in regret. "It didn't occur to me to go back to the other Fail-Safe place to look for the starter. I thought it was in China Basin. That's why I was there."

So Tony had attempted to steal the second starter, but he hadn't succeeded. That meant somebody else had it.

"I most sincerely wish," said Tony, "that I had thought to go to the other place."

He certainly looked sincere. If I ever saw naked greed on anyone's face, it was all over Tony's. "But how did you know about the second warehouse?" I asked.

He shrugged again. "I bribed someone at Fail-Safe."

"Well, tell me something else. How did a nice boy like you learn how to burgle?"

"That's the easiest part of all. You don't own a building that needs security systems without learning how to disable them. Have you ever dealt with any burglar-alarm people? They're always careful to tell you how a burglar can disable their cheaper systems so you'll buy the more expensive ones. Then, of course, they have to tell you how those can be disabled, too. It's not worth it for most burglars, but it was for me. You can't know what having that starter in my bread did for me. Or—I guess you can. You've tasted the bread.''

I just nodded, not willing, even as mad as I was, to tell him I didn't think it made much difference.

"Rebecca, listen to me.''

I listened.

"I've got to ask you something. Please don't turn me in.''

"Don't turn you in? Look at my best suit.'' I pointed to the doughy heap on the floor.

"I'm sorry about that. Genuinely sorry. I'll buy you a new suit—I'll buy you as many suits as you want—''

"Mr. Tosi. Please.''

He flushed. "I apologize. I wasn't offering you a bribe. I mean, I guess it sounded that way, but I kind of got carried away. Listen, what good would it do to turn me in? I've had that starter for two years.''

"It's Anita's.''

"It doesn't exist anymore. It's all mixed up with my starter. I can't return it, and no harm was really done by my having it.''

"I don't think Anita would see it that way.'' I gathered up my purse and stood up. "I advise you to work on controlling your temper.''

"Listen, I'm sorry—you can't imagine. . . .''

I left him carrying on that way, fully intending to tell the cops what I knew. He'd burgled and tried to burgle a second time and nearly killed me in an entirely undignified way. What if Rob had had to write a story headed SOURDOUGH LAWYER SMOTHERS IN DOUGH TROUGH? What if my mom and dad had had to read it? What if I never found another black suit on sale for half price? Being a city girl, I'd never seen any wet hens, but I could sympathize with them.

I stormed into my office in my oversize white dress, hair still streaming, and stopped Kruzick before he could speak. "Open your mouth and I shove your typewriter in it.''

He nodded, grasping the urgency of the situation, and held up two fingers. Then he held up one finger and dialed an imaginary phone. Then two fingers, embracing an imaginary lover and puckering up in a pseudo-kiss.

I got it: The first word was "call" and the second was "Rob." Seeing my comprehending look, he touched his nose in the charades sign for "You got it, boss." I liked that way of communicating with him. If only I could frighten him into permanent muteness.

Chris's door was closed, which meant she was with a client, so I went straight into my office and called Rob. "I know where the starter is."

If I'd hoped to surprise him, I was disappointed. "Okay," he said. "I'm on deadline." And he hung up.

What was this? I called back and asked him.

"I'm on deadline, Rebecca. I just called to let you know where the starter was, but you already know. So let's talk later, okay?" He hung up again.

My dialing finger was getting worn out, but I wasn't going to stop now. When I had him on the line, I said, "Something tells me we're talking at cross-purposes."

"Dammit, not now. I gave Alan the message." And for the third time in a row, the love of my life hung up on me. Not only hung up on me, but left me to the tender mercies of my antic secretary. Feeling a little like Job, I considered the possibilities. I could wait until his deadline was past. I could burst into tears and suffer Kruzick's idea of sympathy— probably a little tap dance to cheer me up. I could throw myself to the cruel pavement of the Financial District. Or I could pull myself together and beard the lion I called my employee.

There was no question what Today's Action Woman would do. As for me, I walked to the window and contemplated death by defenestration. And not necessarily my own—there was more than one way to get rid of an uppity secretary.

In the end, maturity won out. I went back to the reception area and stood in front of Kruzick's desk, tapping my foot till he finished the personal phone call that momentarily had his attention.

"Why," I said, "didn't you tell me Rob left a message?"

He pointed to his closed lips and shrugged.

"You may speak now, Alan."

"Arf."

I picked up the phone book and threw it at him. Just like that, without giving it a thought. I didn't even realize I'd done it until it was over.

By that time, the missile had caught Alan satisfactorily in the chest, causing a delicious "oof," and he had fallen over backward, chair and all. The phone had also started to ring, so I picked it up. "I'm sorry—Mr. Kruzick isn't taking calls just now."

"Rebecca?" It was Rob. "Sorry I couldn't talk, but I had about two paragraphs to go on the lead story. But anyhow, you know about that."

"I've got the funniest feeling I don't."

"I guess I misunderstood you. Listen to this—Sally had an assistant at Plaza Bakery, and she's agreed to keep the bakery going until the estate is settled. So she went in this morning to bake, and she opened the freezer to get something. It's normally kept locked, and no one had opened it since Sally was killed. Guess what she found there?"

"Rob, I'm not in the mood for games."

"Come on, don't be mad—I just can't talk on deadline, that's all. It was nothing personal."

"Rob, can I ask you a question?"

"Sure."

"What was in the freezer?"

"The Martinelli starter."

CHAPTER 19

So either Sally Devereaux was the second burglar, or she had somehow gotten the second starter away from the second burglar, who had then killed her for it. But I remembered the lighter fluid and the matches and the burned ball of dough. Also, I remembered the nasty little theory I'd developed in the redwoods, the one with a hole or two in it. This new little bit of information answered one of my questions. The biggest one. The only thing that remained was to make the two phone calls I'd avoided making that morning.

The first person I called was Clayton Thompson. I repeated to him what I understood Sally Devereaux to have said before she died and asked him if I was right in every particular. I especially wanted to make sure I understood where the pauses were. He said I did.

The second call was tougher—it meant I had to disappoint myself. The all-new, spiritually improved Rebecca who wasn't going to torture children anymore called Bob Tosi's house and asked for young Bobby. "Remember," I said, "when I asked you about your mom's boyfriend? The one who was backing her in the sourdough auction?"

Bobby said he remembered.

"And remember how you laughed?"

Bobby did.

"Well, I've been kind of wondering—what was so funny about it?"

Bobby gave me the answer I didn't want to hear.

So now I had a terrific little theory with no more holes in

140

it. I went over it again and again in my head and I couldn't poke any. Then I typed something I needed. And I went into Chris's office and told her I knew who had killed her lover.

I told her the theory, step by step, and asked her if she could poke any holes in it. "Only one," she said, and her voice had a bitter edge to it. "There's no way in hell to prove it."

"Yes, there is." I showed her the thing I'd just batted out on the typewriter and outlined a little idea I had.

It was close to nine o'clock when we drove to the elegant redwood house in Anselmo. Like so many Marin County houses, it was on a hill and we had to climb up about a hundred rough wooden steps to get to it.

When we were on a deck about ninety steps up, we saw that we were actually at the first-floor level of the house, looking into one of its windows at a cozy study. Anita Ashton was seated at the desk, looking out at us. When she saw who was coming to visit, her bewildered look changed to one of pleasure.

She stood and pointed up toward the second floor, where the front door was. We kept climbing and she met us at the door. "What's up?"

She ushered us in even as she spoke, ever the efficient user of time. The foyer had two camelback couches in it, each covered in shrimp-colored cotton, each attended by its personal ficus. The living room was beyond. Anita was wearing a sweat suit in the same color as the upholstery. It could have been a coincidence, but it was the sort of studied touch she was fond of. She probably had eight or ten sweat suits, all color-coordinated with her furnishings so she'd always look good around the house and never have to spend time thinking about it.

We'd decided that I'd do most of the talking, so I spoke first, introducing Chris.

"I guessed. What can I do for you?"

Anita was leading us down the stairs to her study. It was rigged up to resemble some baronial library, with yards and yards of books lining the walls and looking as if they'd been

bought that way—by the yard. There were also wing chairs
and a fireplace with a healthy blaze in it. The concept was
pretentious, but it was nevertheless a comfortable room. A
bowl of freesias scented it, the only personal touch—possibly
in the whole house. Hiring a decorator took so much less
time than choosing one's furniture.

"We think," I said, "that we know who killed Peter."

Her brown eyes flashed, just for a second, before she
shifted them back into neutral. "Sit down."

"We think it was Sally."

"I see. But why not tell the police?"

"Because we think if we did, they might get the wrong
idea. They might think you were her accomplice."

"Me? But why on earth would they think that?"

"Because we think the murder weapon is in your house."

She sank into one of the wing chairs. "I guess," she said,
"you'd better start at the beginning." She sighed as she said
it, and looked at her watch. Apparently, solving her brother's
murder was going to take too long to suit her.

"Before Sally died," I began, "she said something."

"Before?" Again, Anita glanced at her watch. "When
before? A week before? A month before?"

"With her last gasp."

Anita produced her own gasp.

"One of the sourdough bidders, Clayton Thompson, found
her with the knife in her chest, and she spoke to him before
she died. These were her last words, as he understood them:
'Peter.' And then she paused. Then she said 'I need a,' and
then she paused again. Then she said the word 'gun.'
And then she paused again, and she said 'I need a' and again
she paused. Her last word was 'bathroom.' So what he heard
was something like this: 'Peter . . . I need a . . . gun . . . I
need a . . . bathroom.' A strange thing for a dying person to
say, don't you think?"

Anita shrugged.

"But suppose she weren't really saying 'I need a' but
'Anita'? Where does that get us?"

Again, she didn't answer.

"Not too far. But suppose she were trying to say, 'Anita's gun' and 'Anita's bathroom.' "

Now I had her attention. Her head jerked up and she stared, looking very alarmed. "I lent her my gun. I remember now. Oh my God, it was when she first moved up to Sonoma. She said she heard noises at night. But that was ages ago."

"She never returned the gun?"

"No. I forgot about it till now."

"I think what she was trying to say is that she hid it in your bathroom."

"Why would she do that?"

Anita was a no-nonsense person, so I didn't mince words. "Frankly, Anita, I think she was trying to frame you."

Her shoulders tightened and she gripped the chair arm, but otherwise she kept as cool as ever.

"Would she have had the opportunity?" I asked. "Could she have gotten into your house?"

"She was my houseguest at the time."

"The time of the murder?"

"Yes. She stayed with me when she came down for the auction. Sally and I go back a long way—Peter and I grew up with the Tosi boys, you know, so when Bob married Sally, she and I became friends. We were the same kind of people, in a way."

"Do you have a guest bathroom?"

"Yes—off the guest room. Shall we look there for the gun?" She stood up and led the way. Chris and I followed her into a frou-frou bedroom done up in a Laura Ashley print—bedspread, chair, pillows, curtains, all in the same pink print on a cream background. It was the kind of room I dreamed about when I was a teenager.

The bathroom was compact and had about a million hiding places in it. We looked through the towels in the linen cabinet and peered in the medicine chest and rummaged through all the drawers of the dresser and didn't find the gun. Anita seemed to cheer up during the process. What I'd been saying finally seemed to hit her—that her friend had killed her brother and may have tried to frame her. The part about framing her was the only part that really seemed to make any impression, and now that it didn't seem too likely, relief was coming out of her pores like sweat.

But Chris wasn't satisfied. She opened everything and looked again. Then she shrugged, walked back into the bedroom, and, just as abruptly, turned around again. "Wait a minute." She went back, opened the linen cabinet and removed a box of Stay-Safe Maxi-Pads. She stepped back, startled. "This is it. Feel." She handed the box to me. It was the heaviest box of napkins ever made.

I looked at Anita. Her shoulders had tensed again and something was flickering in her eyes. But she nodded, setting her lips. I ripped off the top of the Maxi-Pads and saw that the box was about half-full. I took out the first layer of pads, and there it was—a tiny little handgun lying in a cuddly pad-nest. Anita reached for it, but I stopped her. "No. It might have her prints on it. We'd better not touch it."

"But it might be loaded."

"Let's just leave it alone for right now."

She nodded in agreement, and I put the box on the bathroom dresser. "Let's go back to the study."

Again, she led the way, shaking her head. "I just don't get it. How did you figure any of this out? I mean, I know about the dying message, but . . ." She stopped.

When we got back to the study, she said she needed a brandy and poured one for each of us as well. When we were comfortable, she finished her thought. "How do you know I wasn't Sally's accomplice? Or for that matter, maybe someone else was, and she just happened to hide the gun in a convenient place."

"I think she put the gun there because she wanted leverage with you. Otherwise, why not just toss it in the bay?"

She nodded. "Go on."

"Here's what I think happened. First of all, here's what we know. Chris spent the night before the auction with Peter, and sometime in the middle of the night he got a phone call. The next day he said he had an appointment at ten. Chris and

I think that whoever made the phone call made the appointment with him, turned up at ten, and killed him.

"We think Sally was afraid she couldn't outbid everyone else. So she wanted to stop the auction. First she tried to stop it by making threatening calls to the other bidders to try to scare them off. But that didn't work. She turned up at Peter's, pretending to have gotten a threatening call herself, took in the situation, and saw that the calls weren't going to stop the auction.

"So that night she called Peter. We think she got hysterical, probably confessed to making the threatening calls, and begged Peter to sell her the starter and call off the auction. She thought he might because Sally really believed that *she* had dumped *him* years ago and that he was still in love with her. She had that kind of capacity for self-deception. But we think what really happened is that Peter just never cared much for Sally. By all accounts—including Chris's—he was a very passive and not very forthcoming person. So when Sally made a play for him, he went along with it but never really got interested in her. He hardly even noticed there *was* a romance, I think. It was simply a fling, and he withdrew from it so gradually that neither he nor Sally really noticed consciously what was happening. But at some level Sally did see it happening and she started withdrawing, too. But she made herself think she'd been the first to do it. It's complicated, but I think that's the way Sally was. She was so egotistical, she had to believe she dumped him. What do you think?"

"I saw it happen," Anita said. "It was exactly like that. Peter never really got excited about anybody—I beg your pardon, Chris. Maybe you were an exception."

Chris smiled sadly. "A minor one, I think. If we'd gone on seeing each other, he probably would have lost interest pretty quickly. I've come to see, I think that his real interest in me was the momentum I started about the auction. That was sort of the glue that held us together. But I didn't see it at the time."

"And Sally," I said, "didn't see that her own aggression

was the glue—to use your word—that held her and Peter together. But the difference was that she never saw it in retro-
spect either. So she thought she could influence Peter.
However, when she called up in hysterics, he heard not the
woman he loved begging him to take her back, but a crazy
lady who admitted trying to stop his auction with threatening
phone calls. So we think he not only told her he wouldn't
stop the auction but also forbade her to participate in it. He
finally agreed to see her the next day to get her off his back.
Incidentally, the fact that he met his visitor in his robe argues
it was someone he knew well.

"I think Sally brought the gun—your gun—to scare him,
as a last resort. I don't think she came there intending to kill
him. I think she tried to seduce him. And when that failed,
I think she tried cajoling, hysterics again, anything to get him
to change his mind. And in the end, I think she did threaten
him with the gun and he tried to take it away from her—his
apartment was a mess, you know. Anyway, she ended up
killing him and hiding the gun in your bathroom."

"I don't even use Stay-Safe Maxi-Pads," said Anita.

Chris giggled at the non sequitur. I think I must have
looked confused. "If I'd thought about it," Anita explained,
"I would have seen they didn't belong there. But I don't see
why she put the gun there. Why *my* bathroom?"

"As insurance," I said. "She told us she had a backer,
and we leaped to the conclusion that it was a man. But I tried
to find out from her kid who her boyfriend was, and he
laughed. He's a very smart kid. He said his mom was likely
to say she had a boyfriend even if she hadn't. Later, I realized
that even if she didn't have a boyfriend, she still might have
a backer. So I called Bobby and asked him why he laughed.
And he said, 'Because the backer was Auntie Anita.' "

Anita looked betrayed. "But, Rebecca, that was no secret.
If you'd asked, I'd have told you that."

"Unfortunately, I wasn't smart enough to ask until now.
Peter wouldn't sell you the starter, so you were going to get
it with Sally's help. You were her backer. But there was a
catch—you'd be stuck with Sally. She'd gotten you to agree

to invest in her bakery if she got the starter, and you weren't really going to have your own bakery, which was what you wanted.''

"Rebecca, you sound so accusing. It wasn't what I wanted, but it was the best deal I could make, and I was willing to go through with it. Why are you coming at me this way?''

I pulled back a little. "I'm sorry. I guess I was coming at you. But Sally saw, too late, that with Peter dead, you wouldn't need her. You'd inherit the starter and you could simply dump her. So that was why she hid the gun in your bathroom. As insurance. If you tried to back out, she'd accuse you of the murder and threaten to tell the cops the gun was in your house.''

"It wouldn't have worked. I had a perfect alibi.''

"But Sally didn't *know* that. That's how I know you weren't her accomplice in the murder.''

"How pathetic of Sally.''

"Yes. It was. But she was a very determined woman. She wanted revenge on Bob Tosi for what she considered years of mistreatment. In fact, I think he was just an average Joe from a macho Italian family who didn't realize what was going on with Sally.''

"She told him all the time.''

"Like so many men of that generation who got their ideas about what the world was like from adoring parents, he was practically in a coma. He literally couldn't hear her. I think he's changing now, but it took a divorce and a couple of murders to jolt him out of his complacency. The point is, Sally was deeply hurt by him and she wanted to prove she was as good as he was in business, or better, no matter what the cost. I expect you can identify with that. You had a similar situation in your own life.''

Anita nodded. "I can, yes.''

"Sally wanted that starter no matter what. She saw it as her ticket to being a person of value. It was literally about that primitive. So she stole it from the cryogenics firm. She heard about the control starter, and it never occurred to her to look for it anywhere but the main warehouse. She didn't have a subtle mind, but sometimes that worked in her favor. You don't know this yet, but Tony Tosi stole the original starter—it's been in his bread for two years.''

Anita nearly jumped out of her chair. "That bastard!"

"When he found out about the control, he bribed someone to tell him where it was and he tried to steal it too. However, the control had been moved back to the vault where the original starter was kept. Sally went unwittingly to the right place and got it.''

"But how could it help her? She was already baking the best bread in northern California—she couldn't just mix it in like Tony Tosi did, for good luck or something. She thought she needed it for its publicity value. And she couldn't have that if it was stolen.''

"She held it for ransom." I stopped to watch her reaction. But she didn't react. She just sat there, politely waiting for the professor to finish her lecture. So I finished. "She got you to agree to meet her on Friday, after she'd put her kid on the bus for San Francisco. You went to her bakery and she tried to extort an agreement to go into business with her.''

"That's ridiculous. Why would I agree to such a thing? All I had to do was call the police.''

"Oh, I think you tried. But she ripped the phone out. Then she gave you a little demonstration—using lighter fluid and a ball of bread dough—to show you what she'd do to the starter if you left the bakery. She'd have plenty of time because the police would have to get a warrant to search for the starter. She'd simply burn it up before you got back.''

"This is too ridiculous. All I had to do was agree and—''

I finished for her: "And later say you'd been pressured into it and sue. But you didn't think of it then. You picked up a bread knife and killed her with it.''

Anita didn't miss a beat. "Prove it."

I brought out the little piece of paper I'd typed up before Chris and I had left the office that afternoon. It said *For Immediate Release* at the top, and the date was February 14, the day Sally was killed. The text announced the partnership

of Anita Ashton and Sally Devereaux in the Plaza Bakery of
Sonoma.

"Rob got this in the mail this morning. She was a woman
who took precautions."

The tense shoulders sagged. Anita's eyes and mouth and
cheek muscles all came suddenly under the spell of the law
of gravity. If I ever saw defeat, I saw it in that face.

"I need another drink," she said, and walked to her desk
to get the decanter. With one hand she picked it up, and with
the other she opened the drawer of her desk. It came out
with a gun.

CHAPTER 20

"This is why I forgot I lent Sally my gun. You see, I have two. Now give me the paper."

"It won't matter if I do. Rob has a copy."

"Give it to me."

"What are you going to do? Shoot us here in your study? How are you going to explain that?"

"Just give me the paper."

"Just tell me something first, Anita. Was I right?"

Her eyes darted back and forth between Chris and me. "Did you two record this?"

"No. We didn't even think of it." Which shows how smart we were.

"Open your purses and empty them."

I looked at Chris. She shrugged, picked up her purse, and upended it. I did the same. No recorders spilled out.

"Okay," said Anita. "I killed her. It doesn't matter if I tell you, because you aren't going to be repeating it. And I'll tell you something else. I'm sorry about it. Yes, she stole my starter, and yes, she tried to threaten me into going into her damned partnership. But, like you said, I identified with her. We were 'friends' if people like us—people who think the way other people see us is the most important thing in the world—ever really have any friends. I didn't feel close to her, but I identified with her. I knew what she was like. Because I'm like that."

I was so bowled over by this unexpected display of self-knowledge that I almost forgot our predicament. She kept talking. "Sally killed Peter, and I killed Sally. Because we both wanted sourdough fame. Crazy, isn't it?'' She laughed. "It might be crazy, but that doesn't stop me from wanting it. I've known for a long time what I am. Some people say I'm driven. You know how my ex-husband put it? He said I was driven by evil chauffeurs.'' She laughed again. When we didn't, she said, "I thought it was rather good. So I'm driven by evil chauffeurs. It's just the way I am, that's all. Maybe I could go get my head shrunk and I wouldn't be, but if I did that, I'd be giving up a part of myself, wouldn't I?''

Chris said, "People say they go to shrinks to find lost parts of themselves.''

"Listen to Little Miss Schoolmarm. I don't know how Peter could stand you. I like what I am, do you understand that? I like being famous and making thousands of dollars for lectures and having everybody coming up afterward and acting like I'm some kind of guru or something. I love it. That's fulfillment, ladies. Don't let anybody kid you.''

"So why do you need to run a bakery?''

"Fame and money are the best things I've had so far, but they aren't enough. Fulfillment and peace aren't the same thing. The bakery would give me peace—exorcise my child-hood demons. That's what I need instead of some tweed-wearing shrink.''

"I don't get it,'' I said. "If you exorcise your demons, won't you be giving up part of yourself? The evil chauffeurs you like so much?''

"Maybe. But I'll do it my way.''

"It won't work, Anita. Once you get it, it still won't be enough. You'll be just as empty as you are right now.''

"Shut up! Give me that paper.''

She took a step forward and I stepped backward. "You've got too much sense to shoot us. This is your house—how are you going to explain how we came to be dead on the broad-loom?''

"That's my problem. Give it to me, dammit.''

"No.'' I stepped backward again and she took another step forward. Chris now had a clear path to the door, and she took it. She was out of the room before Anita could whirl

around. When she finally turned, I attacked from behind—
throwing my arms around her in what I believed to be a
viselike, arm-paralyzing grip. She whapped me with one of
the supposedly paralyzed arms, and, stunned, I fell backward, still holding on to her with one hand.

She whipped around to face me, and then we were both
on the floor, struggling like two galoots in a western, rolling
over and over, me trying to get the gun and she holding on
to it, never getting it into shooting position. We knocked the
firescreen away and rolled closer to the fireplace.

"Hold it, Anita," said Chris. I was on the bottom, but I
could see her standing in the doorway, pointing Sally's gun.
"Drop the gun," she said. Anita dropped it.

"Now get up."

Anita shifted her weight off my body, and then Chris
yelled, "Roll, Rebecca. Your hair's on fire!"

I smelled it just as she said it. I rolled, and as I did, I could
see flames at the ends of my pageboy. I caught the hair in
my hand and mashed it into the rug, rolling over on it, hoping
I wasn't just burning up the back of my neck. I didn't feel
anything, but I guess I was still on fire, because suddenly
Chris was on top of me smothering the flames with a pillow.
The smell was vile.

Anita recovered her balance and dived for the gun she'd
dropped. Chris's knee came up just as I sat up, hoping to get
in Anita's way. Bone crunched against bone—Chris's knee-
cap and my jaw—and I lay back down rather hard.

There was nothing to do but shoot, so Chris did. Or, rather,
she tried to. She hadn't taken the safety off Sally's gun, or
maybe it wasn't even loaded—I couldn't tell at the time. All
I know is there was a very anticlimatic little click. And then
Anita was on both of us again and all three of us were rolling.

My hip landed on something hard, and then it was under
the small of my back, digging in and nearly killing me.
"Ow," I yelped, and reached down to grab it. It was the
gun, of course, and if I hadn't yelled, I would have been the
first one under my back, but I'd alerted the enemy and her
hand got there first. She pulled at it, and I rolled off the

gun toward her, hoping to knock her off-balance, but the gun went off. I stopped in midroll. The bullet had gone through one of Anita's nice walls, but the noise had frozen Chris as well as me. That gave Anita the split second she needed. She was in control again, the gun pointed at both of us.

She got up warily, first on one knee, watching us like a mongoose watching two cobras. "Stay where you are," she said, and sat on the edge of her desk, catching her breath. We stayed.

"Rebecca," she said at last. "Don't bother giving me that paper. Pick it up and throw it in the fire."

The paper was crumpled on the floor. I didn't move. The gun went off again and I could have sworn I felt the bullet whizzing past my cheek, but it sank into the wall about two feet to my left, so I guess my imagination was working overtime. However, I took her meaning.

"Say no more," I said, and threw the paper into the fire, wondering why I'd been so stubborn about it in the first place.

"Now stand up. Both of you."

We did.

"Chris, kick that gun over here." She meant Sally's, and Chris kicked it. In one graceful movement, Anita picked it up. Keeping the other gun trained on us, she locked Sally's in her desk drawer. "And now let's take a little ride. Put on your coats, ladies."

We had shrugged them off when we sat down, and now we plucked them out of our respective chairs and put them on.

"Now gather up the stuff you dumped out of your hand-bags and put it back in them."

Like a couple of robots, we complied. I hated the feeling of helplessness that had settled on me when she fired the gun, but I told myself that maybe one of the neighbors had heard it and would call the police. Then I realized that the neighbors couldn't have heard anything. For one thing, they were too far away. For another, there was a dull roar above the fire's mild one. It was raining. I hadn't noticed the rain when it started, but then, the evening's entertainment had been engrossing.

When our purses were properly stuffed, Anita told us to go upstairs ahead of her, then walk down the wooden steps to our car. She was right behind us.

By the time we got to the bottom, we were drenched. "Now get out your key, Rebecca, and unlock your side of the car. Then come back and unlock the passenger side."

I did both things, and when I turned around, I lunged for her eyes with my key. She hit me on the side of the face with the gun. I was knocked backward, and Chris went for her. But Anita had time to compose herself and she gave Chris a more authoritative whap than I'd gotten. She went down.

Anita was hardly fazed. The term *cool customer* didn't even apply; she was a frozen yogurt. She grabbed me by the arm and put the gun to my temple. "Get up," she said to Chris. "And get in the backseat."

Chris got in, tears running down her face. I think she was catching on that Anita was playing hardball. And so was I, but I didn't know what to do about it. I didn't want to die, which was clearly what Anita had in mind, and I thought of pleading for my life and Chris's. I could tell her it was all okay—we wouldn't go to the police; we'd never tell anyone that she'd killed Sally; and she could have her damned bakery and see if it made her happy. But I couldn't bring myself to do it. Besides, I knew it wouldn't work. A frozen yogurt who'd killed once would do it again—twice more.

I watched Chris get in the backseat, and then Anita let me go and trained the gun on Chris as she climbed into the passenger seat. "Now get in, Rebecca."

What if I didn't? What if I made a dash for it and ran for the nearest neighbor's house? Would she really kill Chris? She'd certainly fry for it if she did. Could she be that dumb? I decided it wasn't a matter of dumbness. She might panic, or she might just do it out of orneriness. I couldn't take the chance. So I got in the Volvo.

It was freezing in there and we were dripping all over everything. I turned on the motor and the heater. "Let's go," said Anita.

"It has to warm up or it won't run." While it warmed up,

I tried to think of what to do next, but my mind just wouldn't work. The whap on the face had put me on overload or something. I tried to think of the proper computer term for the phenomenon, and then realized I wasn't concentrating on the real problem. But concentrating had gotten me nowhere, so I tried not to think at all—just let the system relax for a bit.

Finally, Anita ordered me to start the car and go down the hill. I did.

Then she had me turn right and go up a hill, then go back down it and turn left and go up another hill. I couldn't figure what in the name of Clarence Darrow she was doing. I could hardly see anything in the rain, and there was fog, too, but at least there wasn't much traffic on those curly Marin roads.

The way that part of the county is set up, everybody lives on a hill. You have to wind up and then down, and who knows what else, to find your house—and heaven help you if you're drunk. I'd grown up in these hills—or their cousins in San Rafael—and I had no desire to live in them. Give me a nice well-lighted city street.

As we wound back and forth, up one hill and down another, I began to get the glimmerings of an idea. If we ran into a car, I could put it into action. A couple of minutes later, one came at us.

I hit my horn. The car swerved, hit the side of the hill, and nearly skidded into us. It was close enough to see who the driver was, and the minute I did, I hit the gas. I'd meant to stop, having summoned help in a crude way, but I hadn't thought the plan out any further than that. I guess I'd counted on some furious driver coming at us, all irate and full of bluster, mad enough to take on a killer with a gun. But the person in the other car was a terrified teenage girl who looked as if she'd passed her driver's test yesterday. I didn't want to take a chance on what Anita might do. As it was, her reaction was bad enough. She pistol-whipped Chris again. Chris slammed into the back of the seat with a whimper and a thunk and I cursed myself, overcome with guilt and fear.

"Cool it, Rebecca," was all Anita said.

My teeth were chattering and I was perspiring at the same

time. I wondered if I had malaria and realized my mind was
off in left field again. "This is hardball, Rebecca," I reminded myself. "Get back to the mound."

I hated baseball and couldn't think why my brain was playing this trick on me. But it was, and I heard myself thinking,
"We need a hit, need a long ball, a homer, gotta slide over
the plate. Come on, no batter, no batter." I knew I was
muddling things, but it kept my spirits up. I almost giggled,
imagining Rob's reaction when I told him what my tiny mind
was doing just before I—before I what? I didn't know, but I
didn't allow myself to get the idea I was never going to be
telling Rob anything again.

Rob. I said, "Rob knows we came to see you."

"So what? You never got there. You took a wrong turn
and had a nasty accident on the way."

All of a sudden I got her drift. I realized why she'd been
driving us over every hill in the neighborhood. We were
going over a cliff, and she was going to walk back home,
which would be just a few hundred feet if she planned the
thing right.

I grasped at any old straw: "How are you going to explain
the bullet holes?"

"What bullet holes?"

"The ones in your study."

"Like I said, what bullet holes? Did you ever hear of Fix-
All? You mix it with water, stick it in the hole, wait twenty
minutes, then sand and apply a daub of paint. Stop the car."

"Here?"

"Stop, dammit."

I braked on a steep ravine that dropped a long way without
so much as a eucalyptus tree to stop a falling car, a car that
had skidded in the rain and gone off the road.

Anita got out, still keeping the gun on Chris. "Get in the
front seat." Chris did, and Anita stood in the rain, holding
the gun to Chris's head.

"Okay, Rebecca. Drive over it."

I didn't move.

"Drive over it or I'll shoot her."

I shifted gears, not quite as skillfully as I usually do, and the Volvo stalled. That gave me a minute to pray, which I hadn't done since the time I got arrested for drunk driving while rescuing a state senator from a bordello raid.

"Geronimo!" I said to myself. Aloud, I hollered, "Duck, Chris!"

And I slammed the car into reverse. Firecrackers went off as I hit the hill on the opposite side of the road, and I noted with relief that Chris had taken my advice. She'd ducked before Anita recovered enough to fire. We were both alive, and Anita had now fired five of her six shots. Also, we were straddling both lanes horizontally and a car was coming at us. Anita was between it and us, her face a jig-is-up mask.

The other car's brakes screamed, and it started to skid. Anita flew over our hood and landed running. There was a nasty crunch as the other car hit the side of the hill. I didn't waste time surveying the damage. The occupants would have to fend for themselves. Me, I had a murderer to catch. Adrenaline hit the system like a shot of diesel fuel and I poured it into straightening my wheels. Then I let it drop to my gas foot. Anita glanced over her shoulder, staggered, and lost her balance.

I was going so fast it took me a few seconds to stop, but by the time I did, got out of the car, and looked over the ravine, I could still see her rolling in the glare of my headlamps.

CHAPTER
21

The driver of the other car was the irate blusterer I'd hoped for a few minutes before. His steed was a Mercedes, and he didn't like getting it scuffed up. He got out loaded for rhino, but the sight of Chris and me stopped him cold.

She was just stumbling out of the Volvo, crying and shaking as if she were the one with malaria, and my composure was slipping, too. I wasn't yet at the crying stage, but my voice was a mouse squeak. Also, we were both bruised and, in one case, hair-singed.

I pointed down the ravine and squeaked something about an ambulance, though I didn't really imagine there'd be much left of Anita. The guy looked panicked. He was one of those slick, full-mustached dudes you meet at parties who say they're "in real estate," which is Marin code for "Back off. I'm a coke dealer."

"Where's the gun?" this one said, and I remembered he must have seen Anita shooting at us.

"I don't know," I squeaked. "Anita fell down the hill." I gestured aimlessly in the general direction but couldn't think of a single other word to say. I fell into Chris's arms, leaving the slick dude staring after Anita.

He stared for eight or nine millennia, give or take, before he finally said, "I think I see her. My house is just up the road. I'll lead and you follow."

"I . . . no." What I meant was that I couldn't have driven if he'd pointed another gun at my head, but I couldn't say it.

He seemed to take the situation in. "Okay, give me your key."

"It's in the car."

He got the Volvo out of the way, and then we got into the Mercedes and drove about another two hundred yards. His house was much like Anita's, except he had tan couches instead of shrimp ones. Everyone in San Anselmo must have the same decorator.

Chris and I sank into the couches, numb, staring into space, while he made phone calls and poured brandy. When we could hear the reassuring sound of sirens and had help on the way to our bloodstreams, our host said, "I'm Michael Watt. Do you want to call anybody?"

I did. I wanted Rob, but I didn't want the working Rob, with a photographer in tow and his mind on getting a story. So I shook my head. Chris didn't answer at all. She seemed to be in mild shock.

But pretty soon feeling returned to our fingertips and brain cells, and cops came in to get our stories, and I did bestir myself to call Rob. I didn't ask him to join us; I just told him what had happened and said I was going to spend the night at Chris's. Then I called Mickey and told her to call Mom and Dad—I didn't have the strength.

I didn't want to see or be with anyone but Chris that night—I think this is often the way with people who've been through a disaster together. But I couldn't drive to her house.

We ended up checking into a motel. We could have gone to my parents' house, which was near enough, but on the other hand, we couldn't have. Not in our condition.

Before I sank into my rented bed, I made one more phone call—to Rob, who was still at the *Chronicle*, still batting out his story, to let him know where we were, and to find out something. I had to know if Anita was dead. Miraculously, she wasn't. But she had a broken neck and wasn't expected to live.

She did live, though, and is currently awaiting trial for the murder of Sally Devereaux. She is paralyzed from the neck down and will have to stand trial in a wheelchair. If there is such a thing as reincarnation, I hope she will be spared her evil chauffeurs the next time around.

Rob, of course, was furious that we didn't take him with us to Anita's, brushing aside our explanation that we felt the presence of a reporter might have been inhibiting. I expect he'll forgive me sometime in the next century or so.

My mom wrung her hands and cried, but my dad just hugged me, which was what I needed.

Mickey took everything in stride, and Kruzick confined his remarks to my new hairstyle. My workaday pageboy, gutted by fire, had to be exchanged for a do that he said would have looked good on John Travolta. For about a week after I got it, he discoed around the office every time I came in.

Tony Tosi arrived at my office one day with a giant gift box from I. Magnin. It proved to contain a black gabardine suit, which I exchanged for one that cost half as much plus a new rose-colored one for spring. I bought a frilly pink blouse to go with the rose one, hoping it would distract from the Saturday Night Fever look. Tony didn't bring up the matter of the starter, but he looked at me so wistfully I said I'd think about it before turning him in.

In fact, I discussed it with Chris. "Have you got any proof?" she asked.

"No. I just made the accusation and he confirmed it."

"Then it's really your word against his."

"If he denied it, yes."

"That starter won't do Anita any good now."

"But if he hadn't taken it, Sally might not have been killed."

"You don't know that. I don't really think anything could have stopped what happened. Why don't you just let it be?"

That went against my legal-eagle grain, but I didn't honestly think Tony was a criminal at heart. On the other hand, I didn't want him to think he'd gotten away with something. I decided to let it go, on the condition that he sign a full confession, which I would lock in a safe-deposit box. I told him it would stay there till I died, with instructions that it be destroyed if I did, unless I found out he'd been involved in further criminal activity. Of course the statute of limitations on the burglary would run out soon, but the confession could embarrass Tony any time it came to light. He signed it gladly. I think he was genuinely penitent and happy to have it as a reminder to stay clean.

Clayton Thompson went back to New York, told his wife he wanted a divorce, quit Conglomerate Foods, and moved to San Francisco to start a bakery—one that does not specialize in sourdough. From all reports, he and Ricky are very happy, once again proving what they say about ill winds.

Since it turned out Clayton never knew Peter before the auction, and since we know that Peter was killed by his ex-girlfriend rather than a gay lover, I think it's safe to say that Peter wasn't bisexual. He was attracted, in his way, both to Sally and Chris, so I guess you'd say he was heterosexual in a limited way. As Chris put it the day he died, he was distant—distant from all his fellow human beings. I've known other people like him—New Englanders, mostly, and one, a roommate I had in college, who was English. He didn't gossip, he didn't volunteer information, and he liked knowing things that other people didn't know, I think; he was just a very private person. If he had a passion, I believe it was maintaining his separateness from the rest of us.

The week after Peter's death, Chris went home to Virginia for a few days. She said something about it being the season for the dogwoods and the redbuds, but I think once she'd found Peter's killer, she simply needed a mourning period.

When she got back, Bob Tosi, who'd been phoning every day, was finally able to ask her to lunch. To my surprise, she accepted. They've been dating ever since, and Bob is getting smarter every day. He even joined a men's group, the kind where guys sit around and discuss how insensitive they've been to the needs of women. I thought that was a bit much, but at least it showed sincerity. Eventually, Tony and Bob made up, too.

I think Anita was right when she said she and Sally were a lot alike, but in a way she and Tony were, too. They'd always suffered from the feeling that they weren't as good as their siblings. It's too late for Anita, but I think Tony has a good chance of getting over it.

As for me, I'm more confused than ever. I've spent a lot of time lately thinking about what philosophers call the nature of reality, though really it's the nature of illusion that has my attention. I had just watched a bunch of people turn a frozen doughball into a reason for committing burglary and murder. But the crime they were really guilty of was fraud. Clayton Thompson had wanted to defraud people into believing he was just like everyone else in his circle. Sally, Anita, and Tony had wanted to defraud themselves into believing they were different, they were special, they were better. Or anyway, just as good. They probably *were* just as good, or at least capable of being just as good, but they'd hung their value on a doughball. When you thought about it, it was nuts. Then there's Rob—to him, a story feels like real life. I don't think it'll always be that way, but that's the way it is now.

And of course there's Rebecca. Does *she* kid herself? Why does she think she's too good to spend a night in jail? Why shouldn't a Jewish feminist lawyer, as she's so fond of calling herself, have to bear all the hardships anyone else has to face? Why is Today's Action Woman always bursting into tears like a scared little kid?

I think about these things as I go about my business, trying to catch up on all the work I didn't do while I was out being Today's Action Woman and also trying to handle all the new clients I got as a result of the publicity. Which brings up another question. I now have a hot practice because the media unwittingly, in telling my story, defrauded people into thinking I'm a better lawyer than others of my age and experience. But am I? I know damn well I'm not. However, when I'm paying attention to my practice, I think I'm just as good.

I have one fault, though—I let things get to me. For about a month after that night with Anita, I couldn't stand the sight of sourdough.

About the Author

Julie Smith is the author of nine mysteries, including *New Orleans Mourning*, which won the 1990 Edgar Award for Best Mystery Novel. A former reporter for the New Orleans *Times-Picayune*, the author lived for a long time in San Francisco and currently makes her home in Berkeley, California.